THE FIRST BOOK OF THE DEAD

Geoff Tuffli

WIGHT: The First Book of the Dead

ISBN 0-9752669-1-8

PRINTED IN THE UNITED STATES OF AMERICA

Prologue

I remember the first time I saw the god.

He lay there, bound to the forest floor; he stared up at me with broken eyes. "Help me."

I shook my head.

"Is it not a good thing to help those who are in need of aid?"

"Maybe," I acknowledged, "but anyone who can bind a god can do far worse to a mortal."

"You are in no danger."

"So you say."

"Do you think I would lie to free myself?"

"Yes."

The god looked up at me. "Free me," he said, "or I will lie here for a thousand years."

He looked at me. I hated how his eyes could rip through the buried parts of my soul. "How do I free you?"

"You have a knife."

I did. I drew the small knife my mother says my father gave me when he left for the wars. I took the knife, and I cut his bonds. It was absurdly easy; I wondered why he had not freed himself before.

"I could not." The god turned to me. "I owe you, mortal."

I shifted where I stood, not looking at him. "No. I didn't do it for you."

"I know."

"I hope you enjoy your freedom."

The god said, "I will give you something in gratitude. A Word. One of the Seven as a sign of my gratitude to you. With it you will be among the mightiest of your kind. I will give you one of the Seven, in its purest form, not watered down like those your Seers play with."

I knew what he was talking about, and I felt something cold rise within me. "Any of them?"

"Any of them," he agreed easily. "The Word of Command, perhaps? With that you could become a king yourself. Or perhaps the Word of Unraveling. With that in hand, even the greatest of demons would fear you. Or the Word of…"

I shook my head. "I want you to teach me the Word of the Dead."

The smile fell from the god's face. "Surely another…"

"No."

"But why?" he pleaded.

I looked up at the god. "You said you did not lie. Do you mean to go back on what you said you would do? You said you would teach any one of them to me. Any of them."

The god stopped. "I will teach it to you. But I beg you to pick another. You do not need that one. It can bring you nothing good."

"Is that what you said to Arnomoare Nimasgheld?"

The god shook his head. "You do not know what you speak of when you ask me that."

"Perhaps."

I

I hate demons.

I stared at the heavy oak door. "This," I announced, "is ridiculous."

Behind me, the Sergeant chuckled softly. I hated it when he did that; it was unnatural. No more so than any other part of this business, I suppose, but it somehow wasn't *right* for a dead man to laugh.

"Then do not meet with the Baron," the Sergeant said, his voice cold, dead. Ha.

I flipped my hand irritably as I half-turned from my inspection of the door. "Why Nerine Domain? What possible reason could he have to want me to do this?" I thought it might make better sense if I said it aloud; I was wrong. It still sounded stupid.

The Sergeant chuckled again. I almost asked him to stop, but didn't, as he might have been offended. Then again, maybe not. I still wasn't entirely comfortable around *them*.

The door opened on silent hinges, and a small, thin man stepped out. "The Baron is ready to . . . see you." I lifted an eyebrow at the pause, decided it was irrelevant, and shrugged.

"Lead away," I suggested.

The thin man hadn't moved. "They stay behind." He jerked his head at the Sergeant and the two others with him.

"No."

The thin man nodded. Reluctantly, I thought. He walked into the room beyond, me behind him, the Sergeant behind me, the others behind him. The room the Baron's servant had led us into was opulent, even gaudy. I hadn't thought it was possible to decorate a room only with black and yet still have it turn out gaudy, but somehow, the Baron had done it. Another special talent of demons, I suppose. I would have to ask the Baron about it.

Ha.

As I stepped into the room, the smell of rotted flowers greeted me, telling me that the other man in the

7

room must be the Baron. Not that I had really doubted it, mind you, but it was nice to have confirmed the man I spoke with was really the Baron. Or at least *a* demon.

The Baron smiled, showing more teeth than were strictly required.

I hate demons.

I bowed, sweeping my cloak behind me. "Your Lordship."

He nodded, not even looking at my bodyguard. "I have heard a great deal about you."

"Most of it good, I would hope."

The Baron inclined his head. "So it would seem. My brother was very impressed with the way you crushed that little uprising."

I shrugged. "There wasn't much to that. I don't think they really wanted to fight."

"My brother was a fool not to rip out the tongue of his servant," the Baron commented.

The Baron was right. The Baron's "brother" was either an idiot or a fool. Probably both. Apparently, idiocy was not the sole province of humanity. In response to the Baron's comment I shrugged. "That's what I told him."

The Baron stopped. "I am surprised he did not kill you." He looked me over again, this time appraising me with an intensity he had only feigned before.

"I suppose he decided that he needed me."

The Baron took a sip from the paper thin goblet he held cupped in one hand. "I assume you are wondering at the reasons behind the contract I offered you."

I said nothing.

"My brother in Nerine Domain has over a thousand servants at his disposal, plus whatever chattel he is willing to risk." By servants the Baron meant demons. Chattel were human peasants. Food, generally. Demons, at least the sort that this one would call "brother," were no more eager to risk their larders to possible damage than a farmer to risk his grainhouse to rats. "Do you think you have enough force to damage him sufficiently?"

"That depends what you mean by sufficiently. What exactly do you expect of us? We don't have enough to

8

take over the domain, if that's what you are thinking."

"No. The Duke would not allow that in any case. I merely wish you to make him reconsider something."

I glanced at the Sergeant standing motionless behind me. I turned back to the Baron. "I think we can handle that much, at least."

The Baron twirled the goblet in his fingers. "Just get the job done."

"Of course." I tried to sound insulted.

He eyed me coldly. "One more thing. I decide when the job is done. Not you." *Bastard.* I bowed and nodded. "Of course, Your Lordship." I felt a sudden urge to rip that self-satisfied smirk off his face, but resisted it. I turned and left the room, my honor guard trailing behind me.

Interlude (past)

I sometimes wonder what would have happened if I had found the god a few months before I did. My life, I think, would have been very different.

I suppose it doesn't matter.

I remember the day I came home from my apprenticeship with Kastren Potter. I'd known my hound dog was sick, but I had had no idea how sick until I saw her. She was old, so I suppose I should have been happy that she had lived as long as she had, but somehow that didn't matter. She wouldn't eat; whatever was killing her, it was killing her slowly, and painfully. I could see her ribs, and she didn't have weighed more than a newborn babe.

I fed her a few scraps, but she wouldn't eat more than a bite or two. The next day she wandered off. My mother was weeping.

Grimly I went off to find her.

I found her beneath a hedge, maybe half a mile from the house my father had built. She just looked up at me, barely moved, just a single wag of her tail. I sat down and held her, gently lifting her up into my lap. For a long time she lay there, breathing forced and shallow.

She died as the sun was setting, the red-gold splendor splashing puddles of light on the ground at the foot of the trees.

I carried her in my arms back towards the house. I set her down in a blanket I fetched from the house and I dug a grave by a young oak. It was dark by the time I was finished, but after I lay her in the small grave, I built a cairn up over the place where I had put her body.

I hadn't felt that way even when I was old enough to realize that my father was not going to come back and was probably dead—my mother never said, but I knew he had gone off to war and had never returned. I barely remembered my father, after all. This was different. It left a furrow across my mind, one I knew that I would not soon forget.

10

2

It wasn't much of an encampment that we made our way to. There were no cooks, no latrines, not even any tents save my own. The people of Halbine Domain stayed away from the camp, with good reason; none but the dead walked there.

Except me, of course.

The Sergeant gave me a brief salute as we entered the earthworks, moving off then to take care of one thing or another. The other two stayed with me, guarding the only real vulnerability of the company.

There were one thousand, five hundred and six under my command, not counting the spites and shades that huddled about the edges of the encampment singly and in their small bands.

None of them served me out of loyalty, nor duty, nor even honor. They served me because they had no other choice. They served me because I had summoned them. They were, if you like, my prison, because while I don't think I had realized entirely what I was doing when I had brought them back, they were my responsibility; they could not die, could not go back. I had called them, and they had come, but I did not know how to *un*-call them. I didn't know what would happen if I died; the god had not told me, and I had not asked. Perhaps they would fade, or perhaps not, and if they did not, they would be consigned to an eternity of existence without living. I tried not to think of what I had done; I went on, I did what I had to do.

In short, I lived, because they could not.

The moon was full as I walked past one of the smaller bands. A tattered banner had been erected in the center. I thought it might have been a horse's head at one time. This group was not one of our two orders of cavalry, despite the insignia; the banner was from Before. It was faded and barely recognizable. I doubted if the kingdom it had stood for still existed. Eighteen years of war had destroyed nearly every nation north of the Seticau River. I was glad, in a way, that the last year of the war had come in the year I had raised the company. Because of that we had had to kill

11

humans only three times, but even that still left a sour taste in my mouth.

It was possible that the battles would end someday, but the soldiers and levies of *this* company would never stop fighting. I shook my head to clear it. Thinking about this sort of thing for too long was a recipe for going crazy. I wondered if Arnomoare Nimasgheld had gone crazy down there in what they call the Land of the Dead down beyond the Southern Protectorates. They still sent bodies down the river from Searle, I knew; I wondered if anybody picked them up at the other end. I walked along, alone in my thoughts even as I was surrounded by a thousand and half.

The air twisted in front of me, dust sputtering in frenzied dervish circles. I stopped, sighed. "What do you want?"

The apparition opened his mouth in a wide grin, laughing. *"Your life! Your life! You took mine, took mine, took mine."* He gave a mad caper of glee. *"Take yours instead. Take yours!"*

"I gave you back your life," I replied tiredly.

"Life? Life? There is nothing here! Nothing. I can't see anymore, but I can see you."

I started to reply, but the shade was gone. Like always. That was all they could do, running off, repeating words without, I think, even really knowing what they were saying. I had no idea how many there were that I had accidently summoned up along with the rest. They flittered in and out of existence like so much dust. A dozen, two dozen, three dozen. Who knows? When we fought, you could sometimes see them gathering at the edges of the battlefield, shrieking and capering, sometimes mock charging units.

Never ours, so I didn't worry about it much; not that there was anything I could do about them, had I even wanted to. They were tied to me, but I didn't control them as I did the corporeal dead who made up the bulk of my little mercenary company. I walked on, my bodyguard stumbling behind me. At one of the larger encampments, picked at random, I stopped, asked for one of the officers. I

12

felt him before I saw him.

When I closed my eyes, I could see hundreds of lines coming out of me, life pulsing along them. If I concentrated on one of them, I could feel the one it connected to, I could follow along it to find the one I sought, but it was faster for me to simply ask. I wasn't Arnomoare Nimasgheld, probably never would be; I sometimes wondered how he had handled this sort of thing. Surely there was a better way than these few little ways I had figured out on my own. He had the benefit of a thousand years of study by the necromancers of the Moare ith Ghelde. I had nothing but a few years of tentative experimentation.

The wight came up a moment later. Eye sockets long since eaten clean by insects and rodents, there was little enough skin anywhere on his body. His helmet and armor were worn and poorly cared for. That was something else I needed to take care of. So much of the equipment was old, rotting. His sword was sheathed at his side, and his shield slung on his back. He looked ready for a battle three years ended.

"Lieutenant. We move out in an hour. We're to fight in Nerine. I want to see if we can get there and get done with this before midsummer."

The dead man said nothing for a long moment. When he did speak, I could feel a chill seep into me as he stared at me with those empty sockets. "Why so long?" he whispered. He meant the hour to move out.

"It will take some time to pack up the catapults," I explained. "We might need them this time, and we won't have time to make new ones where we are going."

"Ah…" he whispered. He nodded and turned away. I frowned, then made my way back to the main encampment.

Most of the company was on foot. Most of them hadn't even been professional soldiers. Maybe as much as a quarter had been such. I wasn't even certain that the man I called the Sergeant had been such when he had fought the Duke ten years ago before he had died. A mercenary, I suspected, but he hadn't said and I hadn't asked.

13

The company was not drawn from a single army or even a single war. The field I had raised them from had been stripped and fought over at least four times that I could tell in the past twenty years. There were a few indications that some of the men had come from even farther back than that, though none of those would say so much as a word, so I suppose I would never know for sure. Not even all of them had fought for one of the kingdoms that had made up the Empire before the Duke had destroyed it all. Before the end, the Duke had recruited to his side mercenaries and even a fair number of peasants who thought worshipping demons would be easier than paying their taxes in grain and virgin daughters to their human overlords. I almost felt sorry for them, but it was hard for me to be terribly sympathetic to idiocy.

I went to the horse I had taken for a mount. Like the others, it was dead. I would have preferred a living horse, but that wasn't practical. The dead are slow, they're clumsy, but they don't need rest and they never tire. In a tactical sense, on the battlefield, this is a disadvantage, as a single error in deployment can mean disaster. This has happened more than once to me. Both times we came through despite it, but only by sheerest luck. In a strategic sense, however, this is an enormous advantage.

To begin with, there is no need for an extensive baggage train. Spare weapons, and, especially, arrows, yes, but no food, no clothing. A campaign in winter is a disaster for any opposing force. The company can, and frequently does, march night and day. The times we had to do this were never easy for me, but with a dead horse you do not have to worry about temperament, and one can get very good at sleeping in the saddle if one puts one's mind to it. A man marching can make perhaps twenty miles in a day. A road can increase this, and a forced march can double, even triple this, though troops—except mine—are in no shape to fight after a few days of forced marching. Cavalry can make better time, maybe double what infantry can, but cavalry is even more dependent on good roads than infantry, and a thrown shoe never bothered *this* company.

14

There are ways for cavalry to make better time even than we could; the nomads of the Oatrinennen ith Halanere would each take four horses, sleeping, eating, even defecating on horseback, shifting from horse to horse so that all shared the burden of an armored man. Survive on horse's blood and mare's milk and a limited amount of dried meat, and you can make four hundred miles in a day if you are willing to push your horses to the limit of their endurance. No infantry, not even ours, could ever match that. It was my fervent desire that we would never need to.

There are other problems, though, that no living army has to consider. For example, you would think that having raised an army from the ground, you could simply march off and fight.

After all, it happens that way in the stories.

Crap.

When I had summoned them from their mass graves, a shocking number had been long since stripped by graverobbers. Not all of them, but that only because the most recent battle had been against Baron Chalbine, and his forces, those that had had hands, that is, had not bothered to drag away the arms of the fallen. Literally and figuratively.

I sometimes wonder how the legendary Arnomoare Nimasgheld handled it.

They always speak of his hordes as if they were fully armed. If so, it wasn't from any battlefield; that much I can attest to. Then, too, there is the question of replacements, reinforcements. Digging up graves is enough to make the locals a little upset, and that's nothing compared to what happens when they meet ol' Uncle Mattiere.

Which is understandable, when the last time they saw Uncle Mattiere was under six feet of dirt.

Demons eat the dead, so there is rarely enough left worth raising, but there haven't always been demons, and even the Duke does not control everything—not yet, anyways. The nomads of the Oatrinennen ith Halanere, the Far Islands, the Southern Protectorates, even my native Asperine are all untouched, not to mention the lands beyond those, if there are any. I shudder to think what will happen when the Duke tries marching into the Moare ith Ghelde, where Arnomoare Nimasgheld is said to be if he is still alive, or even ever really was.

Interlude (past)

She was the most perfect example of womanhood that I had ever seen, and her name was the Lady El. She was the daughter of the King of Colophine.

This I learned from a lady-in-waiting as her mistress took some water at the stream, her footmen forming a protective halfcircle around her, the outriders keeping watchful eyes, passing over me as if I was not even there. A boy barely old enough to be called a man was no threat in their eyes, not with the number of men they had.

But I took water from the same stream that she did, and I washed my face as she did, though she had women to help her and I had none. The men and women with her looked tired, worn, and more than one sported injury. A demon, I learned, had somehow gotten into the encampment the night before and had taken nine, wounded twelve more before being driven off. They were fleeing Castle Dauphine to rejoin her father at Freecastle; he was the last of the kings to resist the Duke. Castle Dauphine had been part of her mother's dowry, and she had been sent to there to learn to be a lady.

When the demons came, the Duke hadn't even bothered to come himself but had sent only one of his subordinates, a demon who would later take over that territory as his own and name it Chalbine Domain. It was surely against her father's orders for her to return to Freecastle to share in his fate, but to those in love, especially first love, fools can be heroes.

I watched her from afar with a sort of bemused devotion. There was no way a peasant was going to get closer than twenty paces to her, but I knew then that I had to meet her. *How?* I thought as they rested, eyes catching uneasily in the fading light as they watched the horizon for pursuit. When at last they rose up to continue on their way, I thanked the lady who had been so helpful, and turned back the way they had come, walking as fast as I could.

The next day I finished the last of the food I had taken from my mother's larder, salted pork and beans wrapped

17

in pocketbread with a few pieces of dried fruit. I walked over the field of the dead where they lay about a mile from the still-smoking ruins of Freecastle; the roofs of the town had been kindled and fired when the defenders had been forced to flee across the plain, their fallen left behind as the survivors cursed themselves for not having the heart to stand and fight, and die as the others had.

Better to live, they must have said, then die uselessly, for certainly none who stayed had lived. Not here, where the burghers had defied the Duke, refusing to accept his dominion. I stood on a once grassy knoll, the rounded top worn away to reveal bleached stone. I stood there, I stared over the field. No peasant was going to catch her eye. They were doomed—that much even I with my peasant's eye that was unschooled in the ways of warfare could see. It was only a matter of time before the keep on the hill fell as well, and the Duke, he had all the time in the world.

The late afternoon sun banked on the horizon, casting an ugly red glow over the field of battle. Crows picked at the bones of the fallen, and packs of mangy dogs ranged over the field. I stepped off the knoll, hard black boots worn from the miles I had crossed to get to this place. I walked among the dead, the stench and the worms numbed from my senses by the sense of wonder, the fear that had slowly rising within me like a tide subsiding into a terrifying exhilaration.

I could do it, I thought. *There is nothing here to stop me.* I looked over the field of bodies, and I whispered a word.

The wind carried it over the battlefield, and the crows squawked, startled. I spoke the word again. A third time I spoke it, this time shouting it, defiantly, into the wind. *There was nothing that can stop me,* I thought. *No one. No one at all.* I stared at the field and the sun bathing the wounds of the dead, and I laughed. The bodies of the dead stirred, stood, a few with their weapons still in their hands. They turned to me and waited, watching me with sightless eyes that saw nothing of the devastation around me, eyes that held only me in their gaze.

Before the newly risen dead I fell to my knees and wept.

3

We marched eastwards along the southern border of Tambine Domain, taking care to cross outside of the domain amidst the dry brushland that marked the beginning of the Sóage Waste. I pulled the scouts back sharply along the northern flank, calculating that Baron Bredegemon of Tambine Domain would rather watch than risk any skirmishing so close to what was, in effect, no man's land.

The catapults had been broken down and strapped to the sleds pulled by a dozen horses, and the infantry marched in neat blocks. They did not move fast, but they did not slow, not for water or food, not for the night. I slept fitfully in the saddle, not liking the pace I had ordered be set, but unwilling to let my living frailties cripple the company. My bodyguard rode beside me, ten wights, soldiers all and armed and armored better than any other unit in the company; one of them held the company's standard aloft, the butt grounded in his stirrup, pinched against an unfeeling, unliving foot.

To either side of me rode the two units of cavalry I had put together. They were a patchwork of arms and armor and represented an equally patchwork assortment of soldiers, but all of it the best I could find; I had less cavalry than I would have liked, given the already slow speed of so many of my units, and I had been determined to make the best of what I had.

As morning broke above the horizon we crossed over from the Waste and into Nerine Domain. I dispatched outriders to scout ahead while deploying the few archers I had on each of my flanks, leaving the infantry to march in the protected aisle between. We marched like that until mid-morning when one of the scouts reported a road to the east of us that ran directly into a village. I took a deep breath and ordered the cavalry to pin in the flanks in readiness for the infantry's approach.

The Sergeant looked at me from his position at the head of my bodyguard. "What will you do?" he asked.

I shook my head. "Drive them out. Burn the place. I'll

leave the rear open, and order only enough pursuit to keep them running. This first one is to ignite the barrel and see if fear can do half our job for us."

He nodded.

We marched up the road into the village. When we were a hundred feet away, we could see that a hundred or so of them had laid out a barricade. Gripping pitchforks and scythes in their hands, they looked pitifully outnumbered. They were broken into three lines, one behind the other, and from the one in the head, you could see them shifting uneasily. I almost laughed; they must not have believed whoever had brought word of our coming. The walking dead, indeed.

"Raise the banner," I ordered. The bannerman lifted the company's standard, and at the head of each unit a pair of drummers began to beat out a slow cadence. A flight of arrows, poorly aimed, arched out to fall among the company. Several hit home, but none of mine fell by the side; all merely continued, those who had been hit ignoring the arrows protruding from their bodies or pausing only to rip them out.

Another flight arched over the company, and my bodyguard closed in tighter around me, lifting their shields to protect me from any stray arrows. An arrow thunked into one of the shields. Among the lines of peasants, I could make out more uneasy shifting.

I removed the horn strapped to my saddle and lifted it to my lips, blowing three short blasts. From either side of the village, the gathered cavalry began to move forward; the infantry with me charged from the south.

As the lines met, men cried out in terror, fleeing. A few stayed to fight and die, but there was no way that they could stay the hammer once it had been swung; we outnumbered them ten to every man they had, and unlike them, we could not die.

But most still escaped. The infantry, obeying their orders, did not pursue, but only spread out through the village itself, lighted brands setting fire to the thatched roofs of the houses, withered feet crushing the carefully prepared irrigation systems, collapsing the narrow walls,

20

turning the clear water a muddy brown.

The Sergeant asked me if I wanted the dead villagers who had stayed behind to fight to be brought to me. I looked carefully, but could not detect either approval or disapproval in his voice.

Finally, I shook my head. "No. Leave them. Their sons and daughters can come back later to bury them if they choose." He nodded, and turned to relay the command.

We marched through the village houses, and I drew in through my nostrils the parched black smoke rising from the roofs. The flames leapt about us, but I kept my eyes fixed firmly forward, pulling up my hood to cover my face. Without stopping the company reformed and continued towards Alcine. Though not the smallest by any means of Nerine's towns, it was, I had been informed, without extensive walls or other fortifications, and though it was likely that Baron Sevon had put a large garrison there, given that it sat upon the rump of his western frontier, I doubted that he had enough there to stop or even significantly slow us. This would not, I knew, be anything close to what Baron Sevon might call up, but unless he had been warned, his nearest major body of troops would be at Talmegor and Lega, and both of those days away even on horseback. Moreover, our lightning march as soon as we received the contract from Baron Halbine had been designed to guard against just such a possibility of forewarning.

Night came, and morning, and as the evening of the following day approached, I had the catapults unpacked and set up, lining them there upon the ridgeline above the town. There were fortifications on the ridge, but either they had, in fact, been taken completely by surprise or else they had decided to concentrate what troops they had in the town below.

Whichever it was, the advantage possessed by the heights was one I was loathe to let pass by. I kept half the cavalry, as well as my own bodyguard, below the ridgeline behind the catapults to act as a reserve, while deploying the infantry to march on the town in the morning. They would, I hoped, suspect a night attack if they knew what faced them, and taking them tired and worn out would make it easier on us, and possibly them as well if any of them were smart enough to run; if any tried to escape in the night, it was one fewer man who had to die.

Besides, I thought it unlikely that they could outrun our advance, though sooner or later we would have to change our approach, as once Baron Sevon's host was mobilized, I knew even the company could not stand against it—if they were overwhelmed, there was a good chance I would be caught with my figurative pants down, and this contract, any contract, was not worth *my* life.

The sun rose with morning, and as the company's infantry began to move on the fortified positions in the town, two men pulled open a small gate, and pouring from the gate came hounds, bringing with them the scent of rotted flowers.

The hounds of hell.

Somehow, someway, Baron Sevon had been warned, and now I was paying the price for that fatal miscalculation. A hundred, two hundred, five hundred hounds howled as they leapt for the infantry, closing faster than any common infantry could have done. The first wave hit, and the front line crumpled under the sheer weight of flesh.

"Catapults!" I shouted, and from a half-dozen places along the ridgeline, heavy stones were flung into the fray, but even as the stones were launched I realized the error, for with the melee as mixed as it was, as many of my soldiers would be hit as theirs.

The front three lines had collapsed entirely, but there the dead held, spears and shields and cruder weapons cut and impaled hounds that shrieked with unholy glee as they tore into my units.

The hounds swept not only into, but more importantly around our formations. From the gates came the reason why; a heavily armored unit of men or demons mounted on horses pitch as night charged out from its protective embrace, iron hooves crushing the hounds in their way underfoot. Startled yelps gave way to roars of pain, and the horsemen smashed into the head of our lines, crumpling them. A hundred twinges blossomed in my chest, and a hundred lights winked out as strings of light twisted and snapped even as I stood there staring in shock.

The Sergeant looked at me. He said, "Order a retreat. Now, while there is still time."

I nodded, wiped the sweat from my brow, and shakily gave the order. "The cavalry to cover the catapults?"

The Sergeant shook his head. "It is too late for that," he said in that shadow of a voice that was the one I knew as his. "The catapults must be abandoned, too. There is no time to save them."

I wanted to protest, to argue, but I knew he was right, or rather, that his judgement in such things was better than mine.

I lifted the horn to my lips and sounded the retreat, reining in, turning my mount to gallop northwards.

Ten miles away we rested, crowded into a knoll. My stomach heaved on the ground; the Sergeant stood over me, warding me from the others. When I looked up, he was watching me. "I didn't know they could die," I whispered.

"They were destroyed. They did not die."

"My link with those who fell. It just...snapped. Broke." I swallowed, kneeling on the ground, cradling my stomach. "My insides...turned. I didn't know that would happen."

"You did not know. You will be ready for it when it happens next time."

"Maybe this is wrong. Maybe what I am doing is wrong. Perhaps I should never have accepted this contract, never accepted any of them."

"It is done. You must live with your choices."

I laughed softly. "That is easy for you to say. You are already dead."

For a moment he said nothing. "The choices, the consequences, they never end. Not even with death." He turned and walked away.

I felt sick, and this time I didn't know why.

Interlude (past)

Freecastle fell. I brought my army to its gates and demanded to speak with the king. They refused to bring him to me, claiming it a trick to lure them out, saying that even were my words true, they would never ally themselves with a horror such as me. They said that me and mine were as bad as those they fought against.

Fools.

Shame-faced I turned and rode away, the dead crowding my heels. From the promontory south of the castle I watched as the demons tore the stones from their foundations and, at the end, herded the people together, penning them like animals to feed their masters' appetites. When the banner of the old king was torn down, I took my army away from that place.

There was nothing there for me.

4

"Here." I indicated a mark on the map. "If we move around that group of hills—on the westward side—we can strike behind their lines and to the north. They must have concentrated most of their forces at Alcine, which means any reserves remaining must be in Talmegor and Lega. Probably the latter."

The Sergeant said nothing for a long time. I waited. He shifted where he stood; the rotting flesh reached my nostrils, but I ignored it. "You still mean to follow the contract."

"And the alternative?" I demanded. "We'll never get another contract if we cross Baron Halbine."

"That is so." But the question still hung on his words, unvoiced.

"We will march north," I said firmly. The Sergeant nodded, bones rubbing rawly against each other, empty sockets staring out sightlessly across the map I had lain across the bare dirt ground.

I called the officers to me, and told them what I planned to do. None of them had any word for me; they never did, not unless I asked them. I watched them as they walked away, something hard growing in my belly. They were mine, my arm, my hand. My strength. They were there to do with what I would, and here I would send them against Baron Sevon of Nerine Domain, I would make the creature fear me as none of his kind had every truly feared anything before. I swung myself into the saddle, the leather padding beneath it shifting under me. I took the reins in my hands and stabbed my heels into the bony haunches of the animal I had raised from its endless slumber.

Through that night and two more and the days between we marched hard. I slept when I could in the saddle, eating sparingly of the rations that were there for me and me alone; I was not hungry, and could not keep what I ate down, but there was something inside of me that demanded release, and I knew that that release was only north, where I could hurt Baron Sevon, where I could chew his holdings into powder, grind them to dust under the tread of the army that marched at my heels, that did my bidding no matter where I led it.

By nightfall of the third day since we had left I judged we were far enough. I ordered the cavalry out, and with me I took the remnants of the infantry that had survived the failed attack on Alcine to the south and marched them in a swathe of destruction across the northern plain, razing six villages in succession, moving quickly and erratically to avoid the inevitable concentration of forces that Baron Sevon would eventually have to commit to pinning me down; it did not matter, for I did not plan on being pinned down, even if it forced us to pass aside richer plums than Alcine.

For five days we ravaged the countryside. This time I did not give orders allowing for the peasants to be unmolested if they fled. They might give warning to the Baron, after all. I felt something burning in me as the fire in the burning thatch reflected in my gaze, and my fists clenched around the reins of my mount, watching the work of hundreds, of thousands, vanish in a space of days not even amounting to a single week.

Through all of it the Sergeant watched me, not saying a word.

I dreamed of Moare ith Ghelde, the Land of Death, and I dreamed of Arnomoare Nimasgheld. The broken souls of ten thousand or more marched across my vision, and at their head I remade a world into a shape that could not hurt me, where I was safe, away from horrors I myself had spawned.

On the fifth day, when the peasants of another village fled, a single horseman remained, though the thing he rode was no horse, and I wondered if indeed the horseman was as he appeared. In his hands he held a white banner, and he indicated that he wished to approach. Six of my bodyguard flanked him as he stood nearme, the scent of rotted flowers overpowering even the scent of the dead. Even this close, I could not be sure if this was man or demon, for the scent of his mount masked any of his own. He approached, not dismounting, and nodded.

"You are Aspin."

"What does Baron Sevon want?" I asked.

He paused. "I am not from the Baron."

Fear clenched my heart. "Maorg-mehl," I said.

The horseman nodded, eyes cold, almost without emotion. "The Duke, he wishes to speak with you."

I bowed my head. "I obey."

Interlude (past)

I had been in the old imperial capital once before, before the Duke had defeated all of the old imperial domains, all of the myriad kingdoms that had made up the whole of its might. Then I had never seen any place that combined both beauty and sheer majesty as well as that city; then I had never been to the Southern Protectorates, south beyond the Sóage Waste. It was built on something of the same model as Freecastle, but on a far larger—and not to mention, far more elaborate—scale. The sprawling gardens had been left to rot, vines clasping the walls in a sickly sweet vegetative embrace; Maorg-mehl, Demon-Duke of the Seven Domains, had little hunger for beauty.

I was not there long, but there was one thing that stuck in my mind. In one of the galleries stood a pair of murals that stood on either wall along the way up to the two doors leading into the old throne room of the emperor, when this land had had an emperor.

One of them was of the Battle of Crossé Peak or something like that. It was tasteless and gaudy and full of men on horseback and clashing lines of battle and that sort of thing, nothing I had ever really been interested in. The other, however, told a different story. The sky in that painting was dark, storm clouds rolling over a valley, the foreground a ridge, upon which stood a man garbed in a white robe stained almost black by mud, a broad-brimmed hat covering iron grey hair that hung down across his chest. He was clean shaven, and his eyes betrayed a sadness that seemed to reach through the years to touch me; in his hands was a staff, worn and old; he looked nothing like me, but there was something strangely familiar about him.

I had stared at that mural for hours, fascinated by the strange figure, the sadness in eyes that could touch me even where I stood, three hundred years after the time it had been painted, and only who knows how long before that that it took place. I asked a human servant who the man was, and he looked at me with surprise. "He is Arnomoare Nimasgheld, messir."

I said, "Of course. I didn't recognize him." But I had; I just hadn't known it when I first saw the mural.

Because his face was mine.

5

They led me into the throne room, then left. My bodyguard was absent; I had not dared to try to bluff them through the Duke's guard. The throne room was bare, places on the walls a lighter color where portraits had been removed, embrasures empty of whatever artifacts might once have adorned them. The throne at the end upon the high dais seemed unchanged from what one might imagine an emperor's throne to look like. For some reason this surprised me. A curtain rustled near the back, against one of the walls, and six humanoid figures swept into the room, a seventh behind them.

Maorg-mehl.

He was taller than I expected, and the body he inhabited seemed strangely untouched by the presence of what it was that lay within it. His body was sheathed in a simple black robe lined with red and secured with a chain of gold at the waist. Simple elegance, compared to the gaudy overembellishment that his barons seemed so fond of; his was a more sophisticated evil.

He did not sit on the throne as I had expected him to. Instead he crossed the floor to where I stood, stopping a few paces away. I swallowed nervously; the scent of rotted flowers had been thick in the air from the moment I had walked into the hall, and now it grew so strong as to be almost incapacitating.

Maorg-mehl looked me over, and in response to no gesture I could see, two of the six who stood guard over him crossed the distance between us to stand behind me; he was, it seemed, taking few chances with assassins.

"Messir Aspin, you have had leave to operate in my domains," he said at last.

I licked my lips, nodded.

"It is my assumption that there is a reason behind your depredations. You are a useful tool, and it would be a shame to blunt such a thing without need."

"Your Grace, I was hired by Baron Halbine of Halbine Domain."

There was a long pause. Then, "Very well. I will

30

summon him and Baron Sevon of Nerine Domain and question them." He dismissed me with a casual flick of his fingers.

"Thank you, Your Grace." I bowed and walked quickly from the chamber, the eyes of his Walkers on me as I left. I wanted to curse, but I was shaking too hard as I walked back into the hall outside the throne room. This was the last thing I wanted. I suspected rather strongly that Baron Halbine would feel the same, and would not enjoy being summoned before his liege-lord. I started to pray very hard that he would not take it out on me.

Demons are notably reluctant to accept failure on the part of their subordinates.

A few days later, a servant led me to the hall before the throne room with the murals. As I stood there Baron Halbine walked into the room. At the doorway to the hall he paused, then spoke a few soft words to the guards who had accompanied him. They stopped by the doorway, watching as their lord walked on ahead.

Baron Halbine's gaze swept across the hall, settled on me briefly.

He nodded almost imperceptibly, then crossed the distance to the doors leading into the throne room, passed within.

A few moments later, a thin, tall man reeking of rotted flowers entered the room. His jaw clenched as his eyes fell on me.

He, too, left his escort at the doorway, but he did not cross directly to the throne room, instead choosing to walk up to me. His clothing was of a fine cut, the colors rich and dark. "I will see you dead before the year is done, human." With that vote of confidence, he turned and followed the path laid down by Baron Halbine into the throne room, the reek of rotted flowers thinning slightly as he left the hall.

I waited outside the throne room, unable to stop fidgeting as I paced up and down the hall, ignoring the guards at the one end of the hall and the two bronze doors at the other end. At length one of the bronze doors opened a crack and a servant walked out. "Messir Aspin?" I nodded. "His Grace would like to speak with you."

I was on the verge of panic as I followed him into the throne room. The Duke was seated on his throne this time, the two Barons standing before him with as much distance as they could manage put between them. The servant waited by the door, watching me. I controlled by instinct to run and forced myself to walk towards the throne, standing carefully between the two Barons before the Duke. Baron Sevon looked as if he had bitten into something that had turned sour in his mouth; he gazed at me with hate in his eyes. Baron Halbine appeared amused.

"Messir Aspin," said the Duke, "it has been suggested that your services may still be of value. Do you think this is in fact the case?"

I swallowed, my throat dry. "Yes, Your Grace."

"Very well. You are familiar with the city of Tona?"

I blinked. Tona? "Y—yes, Your Grace." What was he suggesting? Tona was on the other side of the Sóage Waste. Why, it couldn't be more than thirty miles from Capiné at the northern edge of the Southern Protectorates…my eyes widened as I realized what he intended.

His face still utterly without expression, the Duke waited until my face settled. "You will leave your company behind. A Navigator will be retained to take you across the Sóage Waste to Tona. There, I believe, you will find sufficient forces inside the city itself to overwhelm it."

"Sufficient forces?" I looked at the Duke, uncomprehending.

"Unlike here in the Seven Domains, those in Tona do not burn their dead."

Oh.

I hesitated. "And then, Your Grace?"

"You will raze the city, then march south to the mouth of the bay, taking and holding Capiné, there waiting for Baron Sevon of Nerine Domain to meet you there with his forces. The ships carrying his forces need the port at Capiné secured before they can land. He will give you new instructions when he relieves you."

I would be utterly defenseless until I reached Tona,

out of all contact with my only base of power, and forced to do again what I had sworn never to do again. Worse, those I would be fighting against were human, not demon. I didn't want to ask what would happen if I refused the contract.

His eyes watching me, this time Baron Sevon of Nerine Domain was smiling.

6

Seers will talk about the Seven Words of Power as if there were, in truth, only seven. There are more; the Seven are simply the most powerful of those that humankind have managed to acquire over the centuries, by gift from one of the gods, by happenstance, or by bribery or trade with god or demon.

The Words of Power have power over the world because they are the words of being; if you say something in the language of power, it will happen. The gods and demons speak in it as their own language. The difference is that the gods may lie while demons cannot. A god can say, "The sky is purple," and it will *become* purple. A demon can't, simply because it can't *say* a thing it knows to be untrue.

This isn't to say that demons are powerless compared to gods. In spite of—or perhaps because of—their limitations, they are the unparalleled masters of the arts of trickery, illusion, suggestion, perception and seduction.

You have to be very careful that what you *think* a demon has said is what it in fact has said.

The servant led me out to the old parade ground where they had instructed me to leave the company. The servant bowed as we walked onto the field. "Messir, His Grace desires that you be ready to leave in an hour. He is most impatient, messir. The Navigator will meet you at Totine in Halbine Domain."

I nodded and dismissed him, then turned and walked into the silent ranks of the dead that were, without exception, exactly as I had left them.

I found the Sergeant and told him what had happened. He waited until I had finished, then said with a peculiar emphasis, "What do you wish the company to do?"

I stared at him. "You would really do it, wouldn't you? Attack the Duke? Even though you know it to be futile?"

He said nothing, as I knew he would.

I shook my head. "I'm not going to commit suicide to prove a point. And that is just what it would be. We would be overwhelmed. You know that. And for what? No, I'll go to Tona, and Capiné, for him. Unless I can find a way out of it later." I thought. "But I won't let him hold the company hostage to my behavior." I looked over the company, then turned back to the Sergeant.

In a quiet voice, I said, "Wait for dark, then move out of the city. Go north across Chalbine Domain; it's the shortest route outside of the Seven Domains, and it's the last direction the Duke will expect you to head—he'll expect you to go south and join up with me, probably somewhere in the Waste. I want you to take them west, skirting around the Domains. Wait for me a day's travel north of Gorsau. When I'm done with this business or can find a way out of it, I'll meet you there."

"How long?"

"I don't know. It's possible I may be able to lose my 'escort' before Tona, but I doubt it. No need to hurry," I added dryly. "I somehow doubt I'll be there before you."

The Sergeant nodded, and turned away. I took a deep breath and looked one last time at those I had torn from their graves, then took the reins of my mount and led it towards the gates of the city. Once outside I swung onto the horse, ignoring the stench of maggot-ridden flesh in my nostrils that just then smelled better than flowers.

I rode south, expecting to be shadowed, and I was not disappointed.

A pair of what seemed to be blackbirds kept pace with me in the sky above. Occasionally one would peel off, presumably to report to other, more deadly watchers.

The Duke, it seemed, did not trust me.

I chuckled at the thought, whistling as I made my way southwards along the road straddling Gourine and Tambine Domains until it reached the northern border of Halbine Domain where it split the province in two on its way to the city of Totine where I was to meet the Navigator His Grace had "retained" for me. I wondered if they were bothering to pay him.

Twice along the way I met peasants, who took one look at the two-year dead horse beneath me and the hooded black robe I wore and ran off the road, huddling in the bushes, watching me in terror. For men and women

35

who had given their service to a demon, I found it amusing that they were so frightened of one such as I; the Seven Domains is a crockful of fools.

Several times as I rode south I felt along the thin lines of power that ran from me in a tangled web to the north and west; the latter proved that they had indeed escaped the confines of the city, and seemed to be making their way along the route I had specified. I only hoped they would make it to the rendezvous point.

On the second day following that one that I had left Báuine I reached Totine.

It is hard to believe looking back as I do that until the battle at Alcine fighting against Baron Sevon of Nerine Domain's forces that none of those I had raised from the undying night had fallen.

They were the dead—how could they die? But as the Sergeant said, they did not die; they were destroyed. Or, more precisely, my link with them was destroyed.

When the god gave me the Word of the Dead I took it hungrily, thinking that with that, surely, I was the master of death, that even that grim reaper must now bow down before me.

I was a fool.

When Alcine stood and I was forced to retreat, my conceptions about at least one facet of my world were shattered. I had thought I was master when in fact I was no more than the lowliest prentice boy. But I could learn. And I did.

It was that realization, I think, that saved me.

Totine, like most of the towns and cities of the Seven Domains, was walled. Before the coming of the Duke, came to this place and made it his own, only the largest settlements had any real walls. Once the domains had been secured under his rule and the old nobility killed, he ordered twenty foot walls built around every settlement larger than a village. His reasoning behind this was not defense (for with the Sóage Waste to the south, the ocean to the east, and miles of jungle broken only by the Pourtopaine River to the north and west, none outside of the Seven Domains could challenge him, and none within it

36

would) but rather as a means of restricting the movements of what human population was left after almost twenty years of war.

The gates of Totine were unbarred but watched by a detachment of guards—human, of course—in the livery of Baron Halbine of Halbine Domain. There were three of them, and one of them intercepted me as I approached.

"Messir Aspin?" he asked politely.

I wondered how they knew to expect me, but didn't ask. I nodded.

"The man you are to meet is staying in the Winehouse of the Rabid Hound, two streets down from that one." He indicated one of the two streets angling away from the gates.

"And if I do not find him there?"

The guardsman frowned, and I suddenly noticed the insignia on his breast. I wondered what the Captain of the Guard was doing playing messenger boy. "He has been instructed to wait for you. If he is not there, inform me, and he will properly chastised for his part in delaying you."

I shrugged, not really caring, and directed my mount down the way he had marked. I felt three pairs of eyes on my back as I left, but I did not turn. I chuckled to myself, pulling up the hood of my cloak. It was not really all that cold, but I didn't feel like rubbing shoulders with my fellow man.

The Winehouse of the Rabid Hound was a rambling affair. If Totine had been a port, it would have been pushed up against the dock and full of piss and sweat and sailors. It was just that kind of place. As it was, it had more than enough piss and sweat to make up for any lack of sailors. I asked the man I presumed to be the owner of the winehouse if there was a Navigator waiting for someone.

He said there was, and the silence that followed was louder than words. I didn't feel like paying a bribe for the information I didn't even really want anyways, so I said, "It's the Duke's business."

He said, "I'm glad for both of you." He wasn't rude about it. In fact, he was smiling genially, but I was in a lousy mood. I thought about grabbing his collar and dragging his face down to mine, but remembered at the last minute that my company—and my bodyguards—were almost a week's travel away. I took a deep breath. "I'm going to count to five. If I don't know by then which of these nice gentlemen is the man I am looking for, I'm going to call the Captain of the Guard and let *him* sort it out."

He looked surprised. "You really are on the Duke's business, then?" I forced a tight smile to my lips. "He's that one, over there in the left booth. He's a little drunk," he said apologetically. "Would you like something to eat?"

"Maybe later," I brushed him off, and crossed the room as inconspicuously as I could. The Navigator was a lean, wiry man, with a short fuzz on his chin that either meant he hadn't shaved in the past week or that he was just naturally sparse of facial hair.

I hoped it was the latter; I didn't relish the thought of putting my life in the hands of a man who couldn't decide if he wanted a beard or not. That sort of thing spoke poorly for a man upon whose decisiveness might mean life or death—*my* life and *my* death—in the Waste. He was dressed in an oddly jarring combination of faded silks stained by so many substances over the years that it was impossible to tell what their original colors might have been. The sole unmarred item on his person was the burnished Navigator's Wheel about his neck, and the only kind thing I could say about his breath was that it didn't smell of rotten flowers, though in fairness I realized I should give him a chance to sober up.

The Navigator belched, and he tried to straighten as I sat down opposite him, carefully schooling my expression to calm.

"Excuse me," he said. "I wasn't expecting you until tomorrow. I was going to dry out tonight." His eyes suddenly narrowed, then darted up, looking past me at something behind me and across the room. "You a Seer?" he asked bluntly.

I snorted. "What do you think?"

"I wouldn't know," the Navigator said to me, "and from your expression I'd say no. But apparently those men over there are wondering the same thing I was."

I turned and followed his glance. Behind me five men in hooded robes like mine but white instead of black were staring at me with unconcealed hostility. As they noticed my inspection, one of them stood. The one beside him leaned forward, then gave a sound of disgust and sunk back into his seat, saying something to the one who had stood. The man stared at me a moment longer, then lowered himself to his seat, still watching me.

I swung back around to face my new escort. "What was that all about?" I demanded.

"They thought you were someone they were seeking," the Navigator said blandly.

"And who is that?"

He shrugged. "One of their former brethren. They're Seers."

"And they thought I was . . . ?"

"A Dark Seer," he supplied. He squinted. "Haven't you heard of them?"

I leaned back. "No. I've heard of Seers, of course."

"Back when we had to deal with bosses with only human vices there were a few of them who wanted to call up and bind some of their own demons to fight Maorgmehl and those that had already been called up by that idiot." He spat on the floor. I didn't say anything; I agreed wholeheartedly with his assessment of that particular individual. "Anyways," he continued, "the Conclave voted no—rather overwhelmingly, too, if the rumors can be believed. A handful of these malcontents went off and did it anyways, but either the Conclave had been right in the first place or they just weren't strong enough by themselves to summon up enough, and their demons were driven back. The Conclave was furious, and would have had them expelled, except that that would have put them out of their authority. Didn't matter, ultimately. When the Conclave ordered them back to Heveith Talige to be questioned about the matter, they refused and bolted from the ranks. The Conclave started calling them the 'Dark' Seers, and after a while the name stuck."

He motioned around the room in a vague sort of way. "There are still a few of them hanging around, fifteen or so years later, mostly off down in the Red Hills. This crowd," he inclined his head in the direction of the Seers at the table behind me, "would like to hunt them down, but the Conclave has forbidden it, figuring that there was enough blood on everybody's hands already, and nothing to be gained by adding more. Occasionally a few hotheads come up here looking for them, figuring they'd be hanging out with this bunch that won the whole mess." He snorted with disgust. "Idiots, the lot of them. They figure that since the Conclave has ordered them to stay out of the Seven Domains, that must be where the Dark Seers are, when it's actually the last place you'd see one of that kind." He toyed with the mug in his hand, then brought it up to his lips and drank, grimacing at the taste.

"You seem to be remarkably well-informed," I said, feeling a bit nonplussed.

His fingers went instantly to the four inch medallion around his neck, caressing the burnished metal of the Navigator's Wheel softly. He let it go with a grunt, looking back up at me. "I have to be—for this. The only Navigators who last any length of time out there in the Waste are the ones who know how to handle themselves *out* of the Waste. The right information is worth a hundred swords. A thousand, sometimes."

"Yes. Well." I coughed uncomfortably. "Have you a name, messir?"

"Tomoare." He shook his head as I opened my mouth. "I don't want to know your name," he said bluntly. "I've survived this long by keeping my head down and avoiding trouble. Well, it seems that I can't do that this time, but I'll be damned if I make things worse by getting involved in things I have no business with, which means knowing things like your name. I don't need to know it, so don't tell me. 'Messir' is good enough for now. I told the Duke's messenger that I could delay for another week, and I meant every word, so we're going to have to make up some time if we want to be through the Waste before the storms rise again. After that, it'll be spring at least before even the maddest Navigator would take anyone through there, and I'm no madman."

"Fine," I said flatly. "Where do I meet you, and when?"

"The caravan leaves tomorrow two hours before dawn from the south gate. Be there, or it will be both our hides decorating the Duke's wall, and while I'm sure that doesn't bother you, it sure as hell bothers *me*."

"Not sunrise?"

"Can't. We have to make the first post by sunset, and even as it is we're going to be pushing it close. Normally I'd allow two days with the first skirting the Waste to avoid the worst of the depredations, but we're timing it close enough that we can't afford that luxury."

"I see. I will be there, then." I stood.

"I'm counting on it."

We exchanged polite nods, and I left. I wanted to find a somewhat higher cut of inn than the shabby rooms that were the best the winehouse could offer. I found what I was looking for two streets down. My horse I left in the street, not wanting to bother with getting a stableboy to give him care he hardly needed. I thought it unlikely anyone would be stupid enough to try to steal my mount, but if they did, I would deal with them in my own way.

As I walked into the inn, I told the master to wake me three hours before dawn, then went up to the room his daughter led me to.

The next morning—or before it, technically—I was at the south gate. Tomoare was there before me. In the flickering light of the torches brought by his men it did not look as if he had slept at all, but it was possible that that was just the way he looked. There were, I think, perhaps a hundred people in all, not including the three hundred or so horses. Perhaps a dozen of them were merchants in their own right, the rest being handlers for the animals, private servants for this or that merchant, and a small handful of picked men who did what Navigator Tomoare bid. Surprisingly few seemed put out either by the delay enforced by the Duke on the caravan's departure or the early hour.

I did not really expect any of them to try to protest—Baron Halbine has a harsh hand on his cities, and it did not take a Seer to know that the Duke would be

41

much, much harsher in expressing his displeasure at any dissension than the Baron could ever be.

I sat in my saddle in the shadows, my hood pulled up over my head. I had originally acquired the long black hooded cloak because I thought, at the time, it would be discreet and not bad camouflage at night. The merchant who had sold it to me had been most distressed by my horse. With the misunderstanding at the winehouse the day before I was starting to wonder if my choice had been misplaced.

Oh, I admit that part of the reason I picked it up was simply as a bow to the inevitable melodrama of my situation. It amused me, and seemed somehow more appropriate to my mood in any event.

As the last of the merchants was being marshalled into position by Navigator Tomoare's heavy-handed lackeys, a broad-shouldered man with a neatly trimmed black beard stepped up to me. "Messir?" he said urbanely. "My name is Shaupin. I am the Navigator's liaison with the merchants, but I also manage his special interests." He smiled. "Which in this case means you. The Navigator," he continued, "extends you an invitation to ride with him."

"Tell Navigator Tomoare that I would be pleased to accept."

He smiled again, and I think he really meant it. "This way, then."

Shaupin led me to the head of the line where Tomoare waited on a scraggly sorrel. A spyglass rode in a leather holster affixed to his saddle, and he had wrapped a thin strip of white cloth around his forehead several times, tucking the end into the back. His horse shied nervously as I approached; the gelding did not like my mount. Tomoare looked up. "Ah, it's you. Good. Are you ready?"

"Of course."

Tomoare shouted a few orders at the top of his lungs; reasonable, I thought, given how far back the line extended. Slowly, inexorably, the caravan ground to a start. The pace set by Tomoare was not taxing by my standards, but the merchants were not taking it well. There was considerable grumbling down the line, and it

42

was only the hard faces of the Navigator's outriders that kept the worst from bubbling over into something ugly; by noon two of the horses had expired from the pace being set by Tomoare, neither of them Tomoare's own.

"Should complain to the Duke, not me," Tomoare grumbled.

"You don't accept stupidity from your own men. Why do you wish to accept it from them?"

Tomoare glanced at me sideways. "Tell me something, if you would."

"Yes?"

"Are you always so disagreeable?"

I said nothing.

"If you don't mind me saying so, you don't seem thrilled by this whole venture. Unless a permanent scowl is one of the things your mother gifted you with."

"You think I had any more choice in this than you?" I snapped.

His eyes burrowed into me. I looked away, uncomfortable.

"There are some who serve the Duke and his willingly," Tomoare said at last.

"A prime example of idiocy if I ever heard it."

"I would tend to think the same thing," Tomoare agreed. "Though it could be said that we—you and I both—are doing a fine job serving his whims."

"Not willingly."

"What does he want you to do, anyways?"

"I thought you didn't want to know."

Tomoare shrugged offhandedly. "I changed my mind. I do that now and again."

I looked at him sourly. Yes, the beard was definitely the result of indecision and not hereditary, I thought. "You really want to know? I warn you, it's not exactly the sort of thing you put your son to bed with."

"You're making me curious."

"He wants me to attack the Southern Protectorates," I said.

For a minute he just stared at me as if I had sprouted wings. Then he laughed, but he stopped as he saw the

43

expression on my face. "You mean it? Just you?"

"Just me," I said softly. "For the first part, anyways."

He seemed to consider this for a while. "What makes you—and the Duke, for that matter—think you can do this?"

"It is not complicated. What I did to my horse I can do to people."

He ran his eyes briefly over my horse. I had been careful to pick one in as best shape as I could manage, but it was beginning to stink nonetheless. It always seemed to start smelling after a while no matter what I did. Tomoare pursed his lips. "I'd heard of such things," he said at last. "I've never seen it done, though. There's supposed to be a Thaumaturge down near Narau who can do something like this."

"Narau?" I said, suddenly interested.

"South of it a ways, actually. Place called Boanhogrinbalge, up near the moors. Bunch of them settled up above a village maybe a hundred years ago. Sort of a monastery or something like. Usually they stick to wooden men, or sometimes stone, but this one fellow I heard of was experimenting with human flesh." Tomoare chuckled. "They say he's more than a little mad."

My expression darkened a shade. "I think he would almost have to be," I said evenly.

"Don't take it so personally."

"And what makes you think I was?"

"Suit yourself."

Tomoare reined his gelding aside, speaking briefly with Shaupin, then riding up ahead a hundred feet or so. I let my eyes follow after him, wondering why I was so angry. *Not his fault,* I thought. *If it's anybody's fault the way things turned out, it's mine.*

The hours passed quickly, and as the day's heat turned the air into a furnace, the merchants' complaints subsided until the caravan was silent but for the sounds of the horses hooves on the bare rock and the occasional whisper of wind across the broad expanse. As we approached sunset, Tomoare picked up the pace, and I was surprised that no other horses had died by the time we

44

reached a stone pillar rising out of the rock a dozen feet or more, strange lines carved upon it.

Navigator Tomoare dismounted as we approached it, and with a sharp order to Shaupin, the caravan handlers moved throughout the line of horses, getting the merchants and their servants to dismount and lead their horses into a rough clump a ways in front of the slender finger of stone poking up out of the rock at a slight angle. The caravan fell silent, and I felt an eerie whine in the air as Tomoare approached the stone, kneeling carefully before it as he sprinkled something in the sand before it. He began to speak his offering, the prayers rolling off his lips with the experience of a man who had done it so many times before. I knew little of Navigators and the way they operated, but I thought that not all of the sweat on his forehead was from the heat.

For a brief moment there seemed to be another voice answering him, and Tomoare paused, then redoubled his efforts. At last he stood, the wind having receded to a dull murmur. The Navigator turned and walked back towards me where I stood with Shaupin. Tomoare looked pleased. "Either I'm getting better at this in my old age or they are starting to like me."

Shaupin lifted a questioning eyebrow. "What happened?"

"They gave me their guarantee that the path to the next post would be free for three days. More than what we need two times over."

Shaupin shook his head. "You are an ugly son of a bitch, Tomoare, but then I see you do something like this and remember why I follow such a runt."

Tomoare swung himself back up on his sorrel gelding, chuckling. "You're no beauty yourself. Did your mother dally with one of those up in the Domains?"

Shaupin's face darkened, an angry retort on his lips. "You will go too far one of these days," he muttered, but Tomoare had already turned towards the head of the line.

"I wonder how a demon would fare against one of those," I said as he pulled up beside me.

Tomoare grinned. "I would imagine poorly, or else

45

they wouldn't need us to lead their errand boys through the Sóage. There, the Lords of Air rule."

We said nothing as we rode on past the post, but I could not help but thinking, *For now.*

Interlude

The Seers speak often of the Three Worlds.

The First World, a Seer will tell you, is the world where the unborn spirits wait to be born. They are not all alike, in that place; this much we know. Rather, what differences there are that might show up later are in that place magnified. The Second World is the world where we live and breathe, fight and marry and give birth and die. The Third World (or so the Seers say) is the world of the dead where the souls of the dying gather to wait on the Endless Plains; for what, the Seers will not say, for perhaps it is a mystery to them also.

With the right words, a Seer can call up one of those unborn spirits and bring them to the Second World; if the Seer is able to have a living host available and suitably restrained, the unborn spirit can take over the host. It's possible that the host will fight, and if it fights hard enough, the spirit will either grow tired and leave, or destroy the host's mind and take up happy—and very permanent—residence. What is surprising is not how many resist, but how many choose *not* to resist; it is almost as if at some level, deep down, most people feel safer in the arms of submission than in fighting.

There are other factors as well. The body must be marred in some way; spiritually, ritually, or simply physically disfigured. For reasons the Seers do not claim to completely understand, an unborn spirit called into the world before its time cannot touch a perfect thing—a circle, a baby not born of guilt or shame, a cloudless sky. For much the same reason, a body so occupied cannot be harmed except by clear water or unmarred steel, and they do not age or suffer from the ravages of diseases, though those occupied for a long time may change in slight and subtle ways.

Seers are loathe to talk about demons—you did catch on to the fact that that was what we are really talking about here?—but when you can pry some answers out of them they will nearly always claim that demons aren't evil in the strictest sense of the word. They are

47

dangerous—that much I can personally attest to—but they are not generally malicious in the human sense of the word. They are not *immoral,* but rather *amoral.* It's as if all of the emotions of a man or woman were twisted into a single hunger.

Even pain doesn't even make them angry; it just makes them hungrier. It is quite literally as dangerous to be a demon's friend as his enemy. But despite any of their efforts, a demon *can't* be sated. The hunger can never be completely gone—it gnaws at them continually.

While this means that demons are rarely subtle in their actions, it also grants them a strength and endurance born of a hunger a human could never understand. If you can control a demon it can give you incredible power, but it is an extremely dangerous—some would say suicidal—road to power and influence. It is axiomatic that nobody who summons demons dies of old age. A demon's natural language is with the Words of Power, and as it cannot lie, it is possible to make contracts with a demon for its services with some hope of coming out not too far behind, which means not eaten.

What can you offer a demon? Food, especially live food, will sometimes work, as will the offer of a suitable body for it to inhabit is another.

But if a demon cannot lie, that does not mean that they will not do anything they can to trick the person who called them into the world, and the more powerful the demon, the more likely it will somehow find a way around the specifics of any agreement made.

And what of the Third World? What of the spirits who dwell beyond the grave? What of those unhappy souls whose spirits have been roused from their slumber to march again, to give voice and battlecry again to that air which once lay still at their lips? There are some who whisper about a Fourth World, though the Seers call such fairy tales and foolishness. But they rarely raise the dead as I do, and I have asked the dead of the Fourth World, and they will not answer. But sometimes not answering is as good as answering, and sometimes the answers most worth knowing are the ones not spoken.

48

7

After the Navigator's offering at the stone pillar we continued at a more leisurely pace. Every so often the Navigator would glance over at me as if expecting me to object, but as I did not he kept the caravan's pace to only six hours a day. Shaupin told me that in the deserts to the north, beyond Asperine where I had been born, caravans would travel at dusk and dawn, resting during the day and the dead of the night. In the Sóage, we travelled only during the day. The heat made it a grueling march, but to travel at night was worse than foolhardy, it was near suicide.

The things that haunted the Sóage had little patience for humans and permitted only rigidly circumscribed travel; caravans required guides who could speak their language and knew the proper prayers, and even then caravans could only travel during the day and along specified routes that were marked only by the markers, the stone obelisks towering out of the grit and rock left why some people now long since vanished, for what purpose we can only guess at now. Leaving the path or attempting to cross during the night would not only bring out their wrath, but could spoil the crossing for weeks, as the things who lived in the Sóage had difficulty telling humans apart, and settled for this by exercising their anger on any who passed through—even those who abided by the rules.

I was glad Navigator Tomoare had agreed to take me through. Perhaps if the company had been allowed to accompany me I might have passed through safely, but perhaps not. I was just as happy not to have to take the chance, though as long as I was passing around wishes, I would have just as soon not have been going southwards at all. I had ordered the company to swing around the western edge of the Sóage, skirting the borders of the Seven Domains; I would have frankly preferred to have taken that route despite the added weeks, but I could understand the Duke's preference for coming out of the Sóage.

The cities by the sea, if indeed they can be called that,

for most are little more than glorified towns, are by and large considerably less formidable than those farther up the river. Gorsau lies halfway from the sea to the Red Hills, Shaur in its shadow, and Tarau in its lap. A surprise attack such as desired by the Duke would have been difficult, if not impossible to effect through the western corridor between the Sóage and the jungles of the Pourtopaine River. At the very least, the Southern Protectorates would have been warned, and any forces from the Seven Domains themselves, as opposed to the dead I was to raise, could not be brought through by sea to reinforce such an assault.

That last had surprised me; I had heard that demons did not like to cross water, but I decided that must be a natural reluctance rather than an outright prohibition, or the Duke would never have proclaimed such a plan. Though perhaps it was not the Duke at all. I did not know what the Duke had said to Baron Sevon and Baron Halbine, and it was conceivable that one of those had proposed it. No, not Baron Sevon, I thought. He had looked displeased, as well he might, as it would undoubtedly be his troops that would bear the brunt of those forces that would be transported by sea. If that was so, I wondered if perhaps the Duke was indeed planning on marching a secondary force down the corridor between the Sóage and the jungles of the Pourtopaine River. I felt a sudden chill. The Sergeant and the rest of them would be taking that route, and if the Duke's forces intercepted them they might never reach the rendezvous at all.

Perhaps two days later I stood with Tomoare as he looked over the assembled merchants repacking sand-flicked tents, frowning. He had responded to my overtures for conversation with grunts, and at length I had given up, standing there as silently sullen as the stones all around us. At one end of the camp there were some sort of commotion, and at length Shaupin walked out of it, a puzzled frown on his face as he approached Tomoare.

"We have a problem, Navigator."

"Yes?"

"There's a man missing."

"Missing? What do you mean, missing?"

Shaupin scowled. "I mean one of the handlers we hired on at Totine is gone."

Tomoare's eyes pierced Shaupin, his attention suddenly focused. "And there is no indication of what might have happened to him?"

"I don't know," Shaupin said honestly. "There's a trail of blood leading into the desert, but that could be anything, maybe just an animal." He paused. "Maybe *they* got him. Is that possible?"

Tomoare looked away. "Anything is possible. There's nothing to be done. Is the caravan ready to move out?"

Shaupin's eyes bored into Tomoare. "We're not leaving him out there to rot for the carrion birds." I looked at Shaupin sharply; never in the time I had been with them had Shaupin openly challenged the Navigator. But, strangely, the Navigator did not bite back as I would have expected him to.

"There is nothing to be done," Tomoare repeated.

"Maybe," I said.

They both looked at me, Tomoare a shade too quickly, Shaupin startled. "Do you know his name?" I asked.

Shaupin frowned. "Of course. He called himself Ursam."

"Are you sure that was his real name?"

Shaupin shrugged. "I expect so. What reason would he have to lie? Does it matter?"

"For this, yes."

"What is it you want to do?" Shaupin asked cautiously. I explained, and as I spoke he grew interested, then excited. "Yes, can you do it?"

"I don't see why not, provided he died within a dozen miles of here."

"And you can make him tell you what happened?"

"What man wouldn't take the chance to point the finger at his murderer, even it was just an animal?"

"What if it was one of *them?*"

"I would think," I suggested judiciously, "that would make him all the more likely to cooperate."

51

"Let's do it, then," he decided. Shaupin turned to Tomoare. "If you have no objections, Navigator?"

Tomoare looked like he had some, but he finally nodded. "I suppose it can't hurt. But we aren't going on any wild goose chases."

"Of course not," Shaupin said, and I thought I detected a hint of contempt in his tone, but if Tomoare heard it, he did not respond. Shaupin turned to me. "Let's go."

I nodded, and followed him to where the merchants were still milling. As soon as it became clear what I was doing, they gave startled exclamations and scurried out of my way, hovering in a rough circle about me.

"Ursam," I whispered.

The wind stirred, and the merchants shivered as Shaupin looked on intently, and Tomoare, I thought, with a touch of curiosity.

I straightened and squared my shoulders.

"Ursam," I said again, this time louder. I felt the Word building deep within my throat, struggling to get free. I held it back, promising it its time would come.

"Ursam!" I snapped, and whispered the Word under my breath. But it was enough.

Or should have been. The wind quavered, then died, and I frowned. I turned, and my puzzlement must have been clear on my face. "It didn't work?" Shaupin asked.

I shook my head. "No, it did."

"What did he say?"

"As far as I can tell, he's not dead."

Shaupin growled, and turned to Tomoare, opening his mouth to say something.

"No," the Navigator said sharply. "We've wasted enough time. The...they will kill anybody who leaves the caravan." Tomoare said this loud enough for the gathered merchants to be able to hear clearly, and as one they muttered to each other and looked down at the ground. Shaupin looked furious, but it was clear that there would be no volunteers, and he could not look alone. He looked at me, an appeal in his eyes.

I shook my head. "I'm sorry," I said in a quiet voice. "But Tomoare would just leave us behind if we did that.

52

I'm sorry for your man, but not sorry enough to get myself killed in a hopeless search."

The light in Shaupin's eyes went out, and he nodded. He turned away, and walked into the press. I turned to Tomoare, I think to make some snide remark about his altruism and care for his people, but he was inspecting me with a intensity that I found disarming.

"I've never seen anyone do something like that."

I blinked, startled by the change of subject. "No," I answered slowly. "I would be surprised if you had."

"It was fascinating. Can you really raise the spirits of the dead?"

"You've seen my mount."

"Oh. Yes. Of course." Tomoare frowned, distracted, then glanced at his hands, filthy from the wear of the trail. He rubbed them on his pants with a vaguely disgusted expression. "Perhaps you would ride with me? I would be very interested to speak with you about this subject more…as we ride, if that would be acceptable?"

I wondered why he hadn't asked me about it earlier if he was so interested about it, but said nothing. I shrugged. "If you want."

Tomoare looked up, pleased. "Excellent, excellent! I will wait for you up ahead."

I nodded, baffled, and went to gather my mount.

What the hell was going on?

8

I've heard many different stories about the things that make their home in the Sóage Waste, almost as many as people who claim to know. I'd heard people call them djinn, demons, ghosts and other, stranger things, but I don't know that even the Navigators know the truth. I've learned things since then, which is to say that *I* know what they are, enough to know that the Sóage wasn't always there, that it used to be green and fertile a long time ago.

Why do they permit the Navigators to cross the Sóage as they do? What possible use do they have for empty prayers and dried fruit and salt? What are the markers? I know that they *can't* have put them up, that they are older even than the buried cities lying lost in the sand. For all I have learned, for all that I know, there is so much that remains hidden, buried as deeply as those cities I know now are there.

But we who are mortal and who walk under the sun, we always strive to know what we cannot, even if what we find is more terrible still than any illusion we can conjure up from colored sands that reflect the sun standing still in the skies of our mind.

We stopped again in the evening as the sun shone red against the rock and sand. The wind lay as still as it had since morning when I had tried and failed to call up the memory of a man who apparently wasn't dead.

Understand, I wasn't all that concerned about the man. Despite the blood, I knew he wasn't dead. I hadn't told Shaupin, but twice while we rode I tried to call him up again, each time with no more result than the first time. It bothered me, a little, but there were other things to occupy my thoughts than one man lost in the desert. I brooded over those other things, worrying that the Sergeant might not be able to make it to the rendezvous point if the Duke had indeed a secondary force coming down through the corridor to strike at the western cities of the Southern Protectorates.

Something had slowed or stopped the company; they were still a hundred leagues north of where they should

54

have been by this time. None of the company had been severed, that I knew; nothing would ever make me forget the feeling I had had when those horsemen had cut through them like paper dolls, destroying them so thoroughly that the links I had so carefully forged on the fields of Freecastle lay broken on the trampled ground before Alcine. But something had stopped them, and it was enormously frustrating that I could not know what it was.

Shaupin directed the merchants as they took down their tents and unslung the heavy water bags from the string of pack horses trailing along behind the rest of the caravan. Someone tapped my shoulder from behind, and I turned.

"There is something I need to show you," Tomoare said.

I looked curiously at the short sword at his side. I had not seen it before. "What is with the sword?"

"I'll explain that when we get where we are going," he promised.

I looked at him quizzically, but shrugged. I motioned him to lead on, and he nodded, turning. I followed him past the outriders' picket, over the steep ridge that formed the eastern boundary of the valley Shaupin had chosen for the night's camp. Tomoare did not look back as he led me across the next ridge, and the one beyond that.

I broke the silence. "Where are we going, messir?"

The Navigator stopped, turned. "This should be far enough."

Far enough for *what?*

My expression must have told him what I was thinking, because he nodded, saying, "Far enough for us not to be heard by the others," he explained. "This is not personal," he assured me. "You would be flattered by the price I was offered."

I took a step back as he drew the sword. "What...what are you doing?"

He looked pained, almost apologetic. "Killing you, I'm afraid."

"I thought Navigators were incorruptible," I stammered.

55

"They are," he agreed. "But I'm not a Navigator."

I was a dead man, and he knew it, but I didn't have time to puzzle his words out because he rushed me. I panicked, backing away as fast as I could. He stabbed, and it was more luck than any lack of skill on his part that he did not hit me. I fell to the ground, thoughts dancing about in my head. There was a word on my lips, and I spoke it, not expecting anything to answer, but not knowing what else to do.

But something did.

The man who wore the Navigator's face turned pale as ghostly forms rose about me. He took a step back, but did not drop the sword. He didn't run, and perhaps that was what saved him.

They turned to me, wavering shadows crowding about me, and one of them whispered to me, *"Who are you who calls us? What do you want of us?"*

I swallowed, my throat dry. "That man wishes to kill me."

It chuckled, but it looked at the man who wore the Navigator's visage and said, *"Curious. He wears the symbol of a Navigator, but he is not one, I think."* It laughed then, a faint fluttering sound that made its forms waver. *"He brings no prayers, no salt or other offerings. Perhaps we shall kill him, then kill you too."*

That was a suggestion I knew how to answer. "No," I said.

The man who wore the Navigator's face trembled, and as I stood there his form rippled, briefly changing into another man who seemed vaguely familiar. The man who had so conveniently vanished. "I'll do anything if you let me live," he whispered.

"Drop your sword."

He dropped the short blade. The wraiths hovered around me, waiting to be told to feast on the man who stood before them.

"Why did you try to kill me?" I asked peremptorily.

"I was hired to kill you by Baron Sevon, of Nerine Domain. It's what I do," he added.

I licked my lips. "Have you done it before, then?"

56

"Yes," he answered.

"And what will you do if I let you live? Will you try to kill me again?"

He paused. He shook his head. "I can promise I will not. It will mean few will be willing to hire me again if they find out what I have done, but I will live, which is more than I can say if I do not promise you."

"How can I believe you?"

He trembled.

"What do I call you?"

A desperate hope filled his eyes as he realized that he might yet live. "I am called Moargheld."

Dimly glowing eyes inspected me with cold ambition. *"You are not like the other one. You have little of his power."*

"Other one?" I said before I could stop myself.

"The one who summoned us before, from the south, from the south."

From the south? Could they mean *Nimasgheld?*

I swear there was glee in its voice. *"You do not have a tenth of that one's knowledge."* They began to crowd closer, and their eyes were hungry. I felt a cold knot of fear in my belly. Nothing like this had happened to me. They had to obey me, didn't they?

They gave a shriek of victory and dove in upon me. Desperately I felt for the links between us that I felt sure must be there. They could be broken, I knew, but these dead I had called had no bodies, I had called them to me without them, and I thought that whatever bodies they might once have had, they would be dust by now; perhaps that is all these apparitions were, grave dust taken shape.

But perhaps I could break the link voluntarily? I tore at them with my mind, a dying man's fingers scrambling for purchase on ropes that tied tighter than the executioner's knot closing about my neck. Little twinges sprang through me each time I did, but I had no choice. With a dozen, two dozen hands I did not know I had I took the links and *tore.*

Stabbing pain shot through me, but the wraiths wavered and then vanished without a sound. I fell to my knees, but more in dizzy relief than in pain, for while it had not been comfortable, it was not debilitating as it had been

57

the other time; perhaps because this time I had done it deliberately. I did not know, but right then I hardly cared.

Moargheld was watching me, but he made no motion to retrieve the sword from the ground where it had fallen. I lifted myself to my feet and inspected him. "Tomoare is dead, isn't he? The blood we found this morning was his, wasn't it?"

Moargheld nodded.

A dry chuckle escaped my lips. "Well, now you really do need to keep me alive, whether you originally intended to keep your promise or not."

He looked at me quizzically.

"There is still one more marker we need to pass," I reminded him gently. His eyes widened, and I realized that he had indeed not considered that. "I think I can keep the ghosts off our backs." I considered the ground about me. "Probably, anyways."

"I will keep my promise. You are in no danger from me."

"What about the promise you made when you agreed to kill me?" It was a stupid thing to say, but I said it anyways.

He lowered his head. "I should have let them kill me, but I could not. I am a coward."

I almost choked. In his place I would have thrown down the sword and ran as if, well, as if the dead were at my heels.

Ahem.

But he was serious; he really did think he was a coward. "Will betray me then, the next time someone threatens your life?"

"I do not know," he said. "I have never been afraid like this before. Death held no fear for me until I faced those things."

"Ghosts," I supplied helpfully.

He nodded. "Ghosts," he said, tasting the word thoughtfully.

"How did you do that, taking the Navigator's form? And the other man's, too, for that matter? Or is that your real form?"

"I am not human. There aren't many of us, but we live a long time. I am young, and have only once met another of my kind since my parent abandoned me. Your people call us doppelgangers." He shrugged. "It is as good a name as any other. We have no language or word for ourselves that I know of."

"How old are you, anyways?"

"Very young," he repeated. "Only a thousand years or so."

"How long will you live, then?"

"I do not know," he replied, "but my parent was over ten thousand years, and I do not think he thought himself old."

"Older than dragons, then." I sat back, digesting it. It was one hell of a lot to digest. "Can you change into anything?" I asked then.

Moargheld shook his head. "No, my height, I can change a little, and what I look like. If I do not have someone to copy from, it is not very good, I am afraid."

"Do you always kill the person you copy?"

"Usually," he agreed. "It is safer that way."

"You will have to change back into Tomoare, I think."

"If you say, I will do so, but why?"

"They'll rip you apart if they realize that Tomoare is dead and you killed him."

Moargheld paused, then nodded. "I think you are right. I did not think this through as well as I should have."

Another thought jostled its way to the top of my head. "Why did he want me dead?"

"He did not tell me, my friend."

I looked at him quickly. "You say that easily."

"Is it not true?"

"Maybe. But why?"

"You saved my life," Moargheld replied. "Besides, I am not very clever, and it would be a shame to die at the hands of those others." A faint smile flickered about the edges of his lips. "And it would cheat those ghost-things of their meal."

Not clever? Clever enough to last a thousand years and kill and take the place of I don't know how many

people. I was beginning to think that my odd companion was a trifle modest for even propriety's sake. His shape melted, again taking on the form of the late Navigator. He looked at the sword lying on the
ground.

"Go on. Pick it up. Somebody might notice it missing."

He nodded and returned it to the scabbard at his side. Together we climbed back out of the depression and back over the row of ridges separating us from the camp. By the time we got back the sun had set, leaving only a single red line across the distant horizon. Shaupin glanced oddly at the sword at Moargheld's side, but he said nothing. We took to our tents and followed the sun to its rest.

Interlude

The more I think about it, the more I realize that I've always been surrounded by death, even before I took the Word from the god in the forest. My father, I was sure, was dead, or as good as, at least. My hound dog, too, and all of my uncles. Then, after I left home, I was surrounded with it, first by the dead I raised from the grave, by the Sergeant and the others, later by the places I walked.

Even when I took up the Duke's contract and went into the desert, even there I was surrounded by the ghosts of a people long dead, those wraiths that haunted the Waste and claimed it for their own. And then there was Tona, and then Gorsau, and Searle, and on and on. It was not until that point that I realized that I had never had a friend. Even the Sergeant was more mentor than a friend, and though I felt a deep responsibility for the others, they were never what I would call friends.

Moargheld was different, and there in the desert I found I did not have the words to describe the camaraderie I felt for him, a man who had tried to kill me.

And there it is, of course—the man who had tried to kill me, for I have always been surrounded by death.

9

Two more days passed, and in the afternoon of the fifth day since we had entered the Sóage we approached the third and last marker for this path. The man whom the others thought was Navigator Tomoare walked up beside me, staring at it.

"I do not want to do this, my friend," Moargheld said quietly.

I snorted.

"What if they don't answer?"

"What if they *do?*" I pointed out.

Moargheld paused. "I had not considered that." He looked at me. "I hope you can protect me in that case, my friend."

"So do I."

He nodded, and walked up to the obelisk standing erect out of the stand. He was good at this; if not for the night on the sands with one sword and an angry mob of ghosts, I would have sworn he was Tomoare. He took out the salt and pouch of dried fruit and laid them on the ground, murmuring prayers. I hoped none of the others knew enough to question him, but I suspected that the Navigators were as secretive about their lore as every other guild I had seen. The wind began to swirl about him, and even from where I stood I could see him stiffen. The merchants shuffled uneasily, and even Shaupin furrowed his brow. Moargheld turned back, running.

"They've gone mad!" he yelled. As he passed me he whispered, "Your turn."

"Thanks," I said dryly.

Shaupin and the outriders fought to keep the merchants from panicking, but it seemed a hopeless battle. The wind swirled closer, and I stepped forward into it.

Sometimes the stupid thing is the only thing you can do. I could see them now, ghostly shapes crowding the edges of my vision, pushing up from the rock and sand. They approached me, the lone figure not scurrying away, and my heart sank as recognition flickered in their eyes. Before they could speak I held up my hand.

"Stop. You will leave us in peace."

"You! We will not be bound to you!"

"You will have no choice, if that is what I decide to do. Nimasgheld walks again, and if you do me harm, it will be *his* wrath that you must deal with." As a bluff it was a pretty thin one, but any one was better than none.

But they hesitated. *"A deal, perhaps?"* they whispered. My heart leapt as I saw nervousness dance across their eyes.

"I'm listening."

They seemed to confer among themselves. *"We will let you and these others pass if you never come here again."*

"Arnomoare Nimasgheld will not be bound . . ."

"You are not Nimasgheld," they shot back. *"It is you that this agreement binds, not him, not him."*

I made a show of considering this, then nodded. "Very well. I will agree to those terms." I turned away, and felt them scattering as I left. Moargheld was at my side in an instant.

"They're gone?"

"They're gone."

He nodded, as if this was what he had expected. Ignoring the looks the other gave him, he took his place at the head of the caravan. A moment later, I followed after him.

Three days later we passed out of the Sóage. The land looked the same, but there was something in the air, something in the way the wind blew, that made it clear that we had left the Waste behind. Where the Sóage was all but barren of animal life, here it slowly became more common, if never what might truly be called abundant; twice we saw hawks stoop from the sky to snatch a rodent or lizard in their talons, and once we even saw a dragon pass far overhead.

We turned steadily eastwards, and as we did the smell of the sea grew stronger in the steady breeze that blew off the bay. On the third day after we had made the bargain with the ghost-things of the Sóage, the walls of Tona rose on the eastern horizon, and beyond that the sea itself. Gulls wheeled overhead, and the smells of humanity drifted over the caravan from the town. At the silent urging of the smells of the dyers and charnel houses and unwashed humanity the caravan quickened its pace without any order from anyone.

The walls, like most of the town, were built of baked clay and rose a dozen feet from the rocky ground; the gateway was a pair of heavy wooden doors rimmed with iron, and as we approached they lay open. By the time we draw near enough to smell the breaths of the gate-guards it was clear that the wooden doors had rarely, if ever been closed. On the contrary, they looked as if the mere effort of trying to close them would only result in the completion of their collapse into a pile of splinters and rusted iron bars.

Moargheld in his guise of Navigator Tomoare asked Shaupin to handle the caravan's entrance. Shaupin looked confused, but nodded. Moargheld and I had discussed it before, and neither of us had any idea what was required for the caravan to enter the city. Moargheld had favored simply changing his shape and mixing in with the handlers, but there were few enough that an unfamiliar face would be noticed, and the chaos that would inevitably ensue would only slow us down, and I very badly wanted a bath.

Shaupin spoke briefly with the gate-guards who kept glancing edgily over in Moargheld's direction. Shaupin shrugged once, nodded twice, and at last handed them a pouch pull of coins. That formality completed, Shaupin marshalled the merchants through the gates. Relieved to be out of the desert at least, there were no complaints, and they trudged triumphantly through the gates, their goods (and presumably their fortunes as well) intact one more time. Most had clearly been in Tona before, for as soon as they passed into the town they split off in several directions, most heading down a narrow street I later learned intersected with the town's market and central square.

Moargheld took Shaupin aside as soon as we were inside and the last of the merchants bundled away, and I almost chuckled as I heard the doppelganger give an expansive account of his decision to give up navigation.

Ceremoniously he lifted the wheeled amulet from over his head and put it over Shaupin. The poor man froze, staring down at the amulet on his chest as if it was a scorpion; he was too shocked to respond, and as Moargheld patted him on the shoulder Shaupin flinched. Moargheld turned and left, leaving the liaison to pick up the pieces of what remained of the caravan.

I hoped he would be able to make a profit out of it for himself. He was a good man, and I thought he deserved it, certainly more than Tomoare had.

Moargheld and I slipped into a winehouse on the corner, and as soon as he was in the shadows, the doppelganger's form melted into the features of a stranger. I lifted an eyebrow as the Navigator's beard faded to be replaced by a peach fuzz and dark eyes faded to light blue.

"Another man I killed," Moargheld explained.

"You *do* have a form of your own, I hope?"

"No, not really."

"Oh."

He nodded happily, and I noticed that his new form was considerably cleaner, and it was then that I began to have suspicions that my doppelganger friend was as fastidious as he was modest. After the late, unlamented Navigator Tomoare, it was a vice I found well within my capacity to forgive.

I let a servant lead me down a hallway to the baths. In Tona, it seemed, they were placed outside instead of inside, but I supposed the general heat and lack of snow and (I presumed) rain made this more practical than it would have been in my native Asperine. I shed my clothes and slipped into the bath, luxuriating in the cool water that was a welcome relief from the rigors of the road. I closed my eyes and dozed for a bit, and when I woke I noticed that I was no longer alone; a rather attractive brunette who seemed vaguely familiar was squatting by the edge of the bath watching me.

I cleared my throat. "Can I help you?" I asked politely.

The brunette started, stumbling to her feet. "Oh. I'm sorry. I forgot." Her figure melted into a more familiar form, and I scrambled halfway out of the bath before I recovered both senses and modesty. As if nothing were out of the ordinary Moargheld said, "I was wondering what you wanted to eat."

"You can change *sex?*" I demanded.

He looked at me quizzically. "Well, of course." He paused. "You didn't think I was actually male? I'm neither, of course. Or both, depending on which way you want to look at it." He—she?—shrugged again. "If it bothers you I'll stick to . . ."

"No, no, it's all right. You just startled me."

Moargheld nodded. "And?"

"Ah . . . anything is fine. Lamb, if they have it."

Moargheld nodded and walked back into the winehouse, and I took a few nervous breaths. I was starting to wonder if Moargheld intended to follow me wherever I went. If that was the case, there were going to be problems. Starting with this sex-changing nonsense, and going all the way up to the problem that Moargheld by his own admission had no idea of what I was supposed to be doing here.

The thought sobered me. What I was supposed to be doing here, of course, was to raid the crypts or mortuaries or wherever they kept their dead here piled like cordwood and come out and raze the city. I got out of the bath and put my clothes back on.

When I slipped back into the winehouse it took me a minute to locate Moargheld. He was sitting in a corner, and as I walked towards him I bumped into one of the servants, knocking her down. I lowered a hand to help her up, and stared at her. I looked at Moargheld in the corner, and he waved me over to him. I looked again at the servant and apologized, making my way quickly to the table where the doppelganger sat.

"What are you trying to do? Are you *trying* to attract attention?" I hissed.

He looked honestly contrite, and I almost took back my words.

"I was just practicing, and she *does* have a nice form, doesn't she?"

I stared at him as I realized he was genuinely asking

66

after my opinion.

"Uh . . . yes, but . . ."

Moargheld motioned with a fork to the plate in front of me and as he did he took another bite. "Eat," he said between mouthfuls. "I didn't realize there was some particular reason to avoid attention. You haven't exactly been free with what you are supposed to be doing here."

I chewed slowly. He was right, of course. I still didn't entirely trust his motives, and perhaps because of that I hadn't confided with him. It was even possible he did not know I had been hired—however unwillingly—by the Duke, and if he did not know that, there was no way he could know what I was doing here.

"I have a contract with the Duke," I said finally. He waited, and I continued. "I had no choice. He has people watching me, so I don't know if I can run."

Moargheld nodded as if this was quite reasonable, exactly the sort of thing someone like me would be doing. "And?"

"And," I took a deep breath, "I'm supposed to raise an army here, ravage the city, then march on Capiné and wait there for reinforcements to arrive under Baron Nerine."

Moargheld nodded. "An invasion, then?"

"Not my idea," I assured him.

"How much is he paying you, then?" Moargheld asked.

I stared at him for a moment, then laughed. "You know, the subject never came out. I guess I sort of assumed that since I had no choice in the matter he wasn't going to pay me."

"It would make sense for him to."

"I don't follow you."

"If he doesn't pay you," Moargheld explained, "then you can rightly claim you were operating under duress. If you accept his coin, however, you become a collaborator."

I mulled this over. "Then what you are saying is that I shouldn't accept his coin when—if—the time comes? Not that I'm convinced that he's actually going to pay me," I added.

"Not at all. One thing I have found is that one can never have enough coin."

I chuckled. "And principle? Can one ever have enough of that?"

Moargheld shook his head. "Of course not. But principle and pay are two different things, quite separate." He took another bite. "When do we get started?"

"We?"

"I'm coming with you, of course."

"How do you figure that?"

Moargheld stopped, looking confused. "Well, if you want me to, of course. I could be quite helpful."

"It would be good to have an ally. I wonder at your motives, though."

Moargheld watched me with those strange eyes of his. "I will do all to aid you that I can," he said, and from him, in that place, he made it sound like an oath.

But then, perhaps it was.

Interlude

Arnomoare Nimasgheld. So much of my life has revolved around him, yet in truth so very little is known about him, even if he truly lived or was simply one more myth to pass the time of children by a fire. History or legend says that long ago, long before Maorg-mehl came to the Seven Domains and set them beneath his hand, there was a man named Arnomoare Nimasgheld who whispered one of the Words of Power, and at his call the dead of a thousand thousand years came marching; they say that he made the Moare ith Ghelde his own, and that it is because of his power that none since has dared enter the deep valley high in the Red Hills, even those who live on the mountain heights above it.

But little else is said, save hints and clues of battles now forgotten, of numbers of the dead and dying past all hope of human comprehension, of the man who did what he must though he knew it might damn him to a hundred hells.

I who have walked in the shadows of the Bevagennen ith Gheldrinennen, the Gates of the Dead, and of the Moage ith Gheldrinennen, the City of the Necromancers that lies on the slopes of the that high valley lost in the mists of the Red Hills, I who have walked in all those places know only a little more. Only a little more wisdom is mine, a little more knowledge; but little peace of heart and mind.

10

"They put the bodies in common graves, or sometimes crypts if the dead man's family wants to impress their neighbors enough to pay extra. A lot extra, from what I could gather."

Moargheld shook his head. "Though why anyone should think impressing the corpse in the crypt next door is a good thing I can't figure."

I looked at Moargheld sideways, unsure if he was joking. I cleared my throat. "How far are the crypts from the main part of the city? And did you get any idea if they were guarded?"

Moargheld shook his head. "They are right up against one of the outside walls with another smaller wall protecting it from whatever comes out of the desert. I heard a few references to it, but didn't want to risk sounding too curious."

I grunted. "Ghouls."

"What are they like?" Moargheld seemed curious.

I shrugged. "No idea. Never seen one myself. I've heard they hung about in small bands at the periphery of settlements in some places."

"Why are you so interested in the crypts? The common graves are outside the walls. There'd be more bodies in them, wouldn't there? And unlike the crypts, they're not guarded."

"Hm. How much of a guard is there over the walled off section?"

"Not much," Moargheld admitted. "A couple of watchmen, and they can be bribed."

I blinked. "How did you find that out?"

"Apparently students from the university have a habit of acquiring bodies to sell to the physicians who teach there."

"Why don't they just use the bodies in the common graves?"

"Generally, they do. But the ones in the crypts tend to be in better shape, it seems. The guards do a fair job of keeping the ghouls away from the city, but some get through occasionally and have a feast."

"That sounds tasty. But that's what I was afraid of. If we can get into the crypts, not only are we more likely to be able to find bodies interred with weapons, but we also won't have to dig them up."

"Will there be enough?"

"No, of course not. But we can use whatever ones we find in the crypts to help dig up the common graves outside the city."

"This is going to take some time, then."

"Probably."

"More than one night."

I nodded.

"Where will we stash the bodies in the meantime?"

"I hadn't really thought about it. Any ideas?"

"The sewers. That's where the students hide them."

"They won't bother us? The students, I mean?"

"One way or another, I doubt they will be any trouble."

I chuckled. "Well, then. The first step is to locate a suitable place in the sewers. I hope you don't have a sensitive nose."

"I've been in sewers before."

"I didn't mean the sewers."

Moargheld stopped. "Oh," he said at last.

"Come on. Let's go. Did you find out where the best place to enter the sewers was?"

"It isn't far."

"Good."

The torches of the city guard guttered in the night air, but ironically I think the torches helped us more than them. As long as we stayed out of the circles of light cast by the flaming brands, the glare cast up by the torches blinded them more effectively than the darkness alone could have. Moargheld moved like a ghost, an ironic comparison given all that had happened, but an apt one; he would have been excellent at what he did even without his peculiar ability to change his shape.

We kept to the shadows, and only once had any trouble; a beggar accosted us from one of the alleys, but

Moargheld frightened him away by pulling out a knife I had not realized he had had. A row of rough lean-to shacks ran alongside the wall that faced the crypts on its opposite face. Moargheld moved without hesitation to a stinking, narrow space between two of the shacks, squeezing through it. I pushed through after him, and would have fallen into the gap in the ground had not Moargheld caught me and held me back.

Moargheld lowered himself into the hole, then waited as I fumbled at the edge. As my feet touched the slimy stone of the sewers I shook my head in the darkness. "I hope this works."

"Can you think of a better way? Or any other way, for that matter?" Moargheld asked quietly.

I grunted sourly.

He chuckled, and led the way along a narrow ledge.

We walked that way in he darkness for a ways, then he turned sharply ahead of me, and then pulled out a torch from under his coat. I saw sparks fly as he struggled to light it with flint and steel. At last, the torch lit, he placed it on the ground leaning up against the wall to keep it away from the worst of the muck.

We continued more carefully after that until we came to what seemed to be a blank wall. There were handholds and footholds of sorts, and it was not too far a climb, though the gap at the top was not as large as I would have liked; I began to have serious concerns about getting a body down there, but if a bunch of pimply-faced university students could do it, I certainly could.

When we had pulled ourselves through the gap, I noticed two man-sized shapes standing about a dozen paces from us. They were still, but it was obvious even in the poor light that they had heard us. Both held spears in their hands, and I thought I could see the point of a helmet on one of them at least. Moargheld approached slowly, murmuring something I couldn't quite make out. There was the clink of coins exchanged and a low chuckle following a muttered explanation, and Moargheld came back to my side.

"I paid them enough to shut their mouths," he said

quietly, "but I doubt we'll be able to get more than a few bodies past them before they get suspicious."

"If they do, then we'll just have to silence them," I said.

Moargheld nodded; I don't think the thought of killing two anonymous guards bothered him much.

One of the gate guards fumbled a bit with a heavy iron key, but at last the door was open. Moargheld and I slipped through it, moving cautiously.

I grew alarmed, for with the walls crowding as close as they were, there was barely enough light to navigate in. I started to say something to Moargheld, but he must have guessed my concern, for he patted his cloak. "I have another one," he said softly.

I nodded tersely, and we walked out among the crypts.

"Let's go back a ways," I suggested. "The older ones may be in better shape, as I doubt this looting by students has been going on too long, and it'd be easier to get at the newer internments, I'm guessing."

Moargheld nodded, and we pressed on past the first few rows of crypts.

I'll say this for Tona; it may only be a medium sized town as such things go, but it had obviously been around for a long time. There were a lot of crypts there—more than I could see being put up in just the past couple of hundred years.

We had almost reached the back when I pointed out a peculiar looking crypt off to one side. Moargheld adjusted his path, and in a moment we stood before it.

The crypt was not large as they went, but it was very old. Most of the markings had long since been worn off, and from the look of it, I thought the only thing maintaining it at all had been the outer clay walls, which despite their short stature were nevertheless tall enough to keep back the worst of the wind, and, presumably, the ghouls, though from what Moargheld had said it was difficult to guess just exactly how serious a problem they really were. Not much, I thought, or it would have been easier to find out about them, and if it had been a serious enough problem, I had no doubt at all that they would have simply stopped burying their dead.

73

The stone barring the entrance was not obviously barred, but it was large enough that I had begun to have second thoughts about the feasibility of pushing it out of the way when Moargheld stepped up to it and felt around the edges. His fingers seemed to catch on something, and he grunted, muscles straining. The stone refused to budge however, and after a moment Moargheld stepped back, clearly upset. He frowned, walked around the crypt, and at the back he gave a low cry.

I went around to him in time to see him chuckling to himself as he knelt close to the ground, sweeping away the accumulated sand and grime. His fingers locked on something that I saw to be an iron ring set into the stone near the ground on the wall of the crypt, and after a long, tense moment he managed to pull it out and drag the stone aside.

He looked up at me, shaking his head. "Whoever designed this had a devilish mind. The big stone on the other side is fake; never even intended to be an entrance. Almost fooled me, until I realized that the stone was too big to move without more effort than it'd ever be worth, and I could not see someone going to that much trouble in the middle of a funeral. And I was right."

Moargheld lit another torch as we waited for the air to clear out. Smoke curled from the torch, sputtering on the damp wood. Moargheld led the way inside, torch held at arm's length. The stone was so old it had already begun to crumble into pieces; the chill air had done nothing to preserve it. The crypt was small, barely enough room for the two of us to fit on either side of the bier standing in the center.

Moargheld held the torch over the body that lay there. At first I thought it was, all things considered,
in remarkably good condition, but then I realized that the remains were still encased in the armor that had been put on him whenever he had died so long ago. The breastplate lay slackly over the body, of which there was damn little left. If there wasn't enough for the body to support itself, the spirit would simply be sundered from the body, much like the spites and the wraiths in the desert.

Moargheld looked over the body. "Doesn't look like much, does it?"

I shrugged. "It's as good enough a start as anything else." I knelt down beside the remains' head. Moargheld leaned forward, but there was no way he could have heard the word I whispered to the knight.

For a moment nothing happened, then the knight's arm moved. Consciousness burned deep in eyes sunken deeply into his forehead, and as he sat up, I stepped back.

"My name is Aspin," I said. "And I have woken you to drive out those who have taken this land that was once yours."

There was a long pause, and a slit along withered lips appeared, and the knight spoke. "I am Urgula. What is it that you would have me do?"

"There are others who must be woken, and I would have you lead them into battle again."

"I . . . remember now. Yes, there was a battle. Two came upon me, and I was wounded. I . . . fell. My men failed me. They did not protect me as they should have."

Moargheld looked at me. "A little slow, isn't he?"

"Well, they don't lose any of their reasoning ability," I explained, "but their desires are muted when I wake them. What do they care about food and shelter and love and sex?" I shrugged. "There is nothing there that a dead man might want."

I glanced back at the man on the bier, and I saw the dead man who called himself Urgula watching us, and I thought I saw a glimmer of something that might have been hatred buried in his eyes. But then it was gone, and I couldn't be sure that it hadn't been just a trick of my imagination.

II

We do not ever truly command another; only ourselves are our own, and not always even then. Sometimes, someone will give the command of their actions to another, but this is only a loan, never a gift. Even the loyalty of a demon is not fidelity as such; even that is bought and paid for, and woe to the one who tries to cheat the buyer.

The danger lies in not realizing when the loan of a person's obedience has been reclaimed, and even more, in not realizing when the loan of a person's obedience has never been given. It is not an important distinction; it is a vital distinction.

It took us sixteen days before we had what I deemed to be enough. Even then it was only eighty bodies all told, and that including Moargheld and myself. We had enough weapons for eleven, though most of those were little more than cleavers and kitchen knives. It was enough to take a city, though, or rather, it was enough to take a small town; few would fight, and of those few who did fight, most would run after seeing what it was they fought. Some would die. I hoped most would have the sense to run, but I knew some would not.

I divided the eighty into two groups, one led by the dead knight we had risen the first night from the crypts. He, with the larger of the two groups, were intended to take first the armory, then attack the city garrison and drive them away, or kill them if they would not run.

The smaller group, including myself and Moargheld, would take and hold the gate, crypts and common graves. There were already whispers of ghouls in the city, or so Moargheld told me, and it was that more than anything else that had convinced me to take the city only with the eighty we had disinterred. While Urgula's group was causing chaos in the city, my group would be busy digging up the vast remainder of the graves we had not had time to get to, swelling our force's numbers with enough to counter any sort of resistance the city might hope to offer.

It was simple, direct, uncomplicated. Short of

unexpected bravery on the part of the town's citizenry, it would be enough to deal with anything or anyone we might face.

And so a full hour after dawn had lit the sky, we crept out of the sewers. As Urgula's group split off to the south, towards the armory I raised my voice in the crisp morning air. "Follow me. The bunch of you over there, move out in front fifty paces. Stay in sight, but clear the streets of anyone you come across."

People ran, most shouting, some weeping. I set my face and turned away from the screams, ignored the pealing of the city's bell tower as it sounded the alarm of a city under siege from a quarter it could never have anticipated. I had deliberately chosen a point near the gates. This meant that Urgula's force would be more likely to encounter significant opposition, but he had the numbers—I hoped—to counter what opposition was likely to be mustered in the short time the citizenry would have.

At the gates the city watch held, and as I ordered the dead forward I could not help but be impressed by the watch's courage. I, certainly, would have run, but then they might (correctly) presume that the desert beyond the gates was a dubious refuge at best, and only even that if they were not cut down as they ran.

The dead swarmed over the city watch, and by sheer numbers if little else subdued them, clubbed them with raw bones blistering from poached skin red in the morning light. As soon as the guards were down and the watch's weapons claimed, I positioned a dozen of the dead by the gates with Moargheld and took the rest into the common graves.

Interlude

Whether by reason of my own inadequate military training or some law of nature, I have never once had a plan go exactly the way I planned it. Sometimes has gone better, but mostly, it goes worse. Lack of knowledge of what the enemy is doing is close to being the most difficult problem to overcome, but is often overshadowed by lack of knowledge of what *your* troops are doing.

The more troops you have, the more separate units they are divided into, the more difficult the problem becomes, not by a simple increase, but by an order of magnitude. One of the first lessons, then, is that it is better to have a solid, simple plan involving a minimum number of divisions in your force than to have a complex plan highly dependent upon maneuver.

Flexibility, too, is valuable. Having a tactical plan that depends upon a certain unit being at a certain place at a certain time is a recipe for disaster, and that is assuming that you control the battlefield conditions to begin with.

Sometimes, of course, complex plans are required. When you are outnumbered or outpositioned, such as when attacking a walled city from the outside, sometimes cleverness is the only way you can achieve your task.

But when you are attacking a walled city from the *inside* when your opponent does not even know you exist, most of the above problems fade into irrelevance.

As a matter of tactical consideration, I highly recommend it.

12

We watched the plumes of smoke rise over Tona as we stood on evening's doorstep waiting for night to come in and welcome us into her dark embrace. Urgula stood nearby, as did Moargheld, but more than anything else I wished the Sergeant were there instead of them. In my mind I traced the souls of the dead in those black clouds, and I could not make myself feel the self-loathing I knew I should feel.

I turned away from the ruined city. "Let's go," I said, and guided the rotting mount beneath me westward, towards the waiting sun. *Keep it in sight*, I thought, *and the night will never come.*

But the night always comes, and there is nothing mortal or god can do to change that.

For two nights and a day we followed the sun as best we could. I refused to stop, and by the second night even Moargheld stopped responding to my remarks. The doppelganger rode in silence, chin nodding as he let himself slip into a fitful state of wakelessness.

With the moon overhead we received our first glance of Capiné, high walls surrounding the small city. Capiné was not large, barely more populous than Tona, in fact, but it represented something greater than Tona.

Where Tona was merely a small waytown at the end of one leg of the Sóage, Capiné, for all its seeming insignificance, was the part of something greater, for it was the first of the Southern Protectorates, and if it was, perhaps, one of the least, it was nonetheless one of them; the others would respond to what I was about to do, and once committed, it was impossible to conceive that I would easily get away from whatever consequences the Protector might bring to bear.

I pulled on the reins of my mount. Behind me, Moargheld and Urgula stopped, the doppelganger looking at me, the question in his eyes. "We will wait for dawn. They should know what it is they fight."

As the sun rose from the direction of dead Tona, the first of the armies of the Southern Protectorates rode out from the gates of Capiné. The soldiers of Capiné numbered maybe half of the three thousand I had removed from the crypts and common graves of Tona, but they were all armed and armored; breastplates shone beneath light blue and white tunics, spears and swords glinted off the sun, horses stamped the sodden ground nervously, their riders holding shield and spear, mace and sword at ready.

My eyes were drawn to the front of the force where a large detachment of horsemen waited beneath the banner of the Southern Protectorates; the man at the head rode one of the largest stallions I had ever seen, and as I watched, he handed a tiny piece of paper to a servant standing beside him. The servant took the paper and walked back into the press of men. Beneath wind an the clank of armor and mutter of men I picked out the sound of fluttering wings.

Suddenly, I understood how the men of Capiné had received warning of my approach quickly enough to call on reinforcements.

I cursed.

Moargheld looked at me curiously. "What is wrong?"

"Pigeons," I said shortly. "Someone in Tona had time enough to pen a message and send it by pigeon to Capiné or, more likely, Gorsau."

Moargheld nodded, considering this. "I have heard of this being done. Perhaps there will be more of a fight than you had anticipated, then."

"Yes," I said, disgusted.

Moargheld was looking back at the Capiné soldiers. A frown crossed his face. "Their uniforms are very fine, I suppose, but you would think they could think of something more interesting to put on that one banner," Moargheld remarked.

My eyes went quickly to where he was looking. Three of the soldiers were escorting the one I had seen at the head beneath a flag of parley. "Come on," I said. "Let's go see what they want."

I shook the reins, and my mount lumbered to motion, hoofs clattering on the hard ground as I rode towards

80

them to a point midway between our two armies. Moargheld hesitated for a moment, then followed after. The four horsemen from Capiné waited for us to join them at the midpoint. As I slowed I pulled my mount sideways to them. Moargheld paced his own steed behind me, eyeing the others curiously.

"Good morning, messir," I said.

The man at the head of the others frowned. Iron grey hair touched off a neatly trimmed beard of the same color, all framing a set of eyes of the same hard color. His armor was impressive, all fluted grooves and flourishes, the none of it detracting from the functionality. "I wish I could say the same, but given the presence of a strange army just come from Tona, I find it difficult to rouse similar sentiment. Who are you?"

"A messenger," I replied. "Delivering a message of utmost importance to the people of Capiné."

"And what is this message?"

I smiled. "Very simple, really. Capiné is now under the protection of Duke Maorg-mehl of the Seven Domains. I am here to inform you that the military forces of the Southern Protectorates are no longer welcome here."

The grey-bearded man nodded. "You will try. But we will not die alone."

"No, I think otherwise. Look again."

For the first time the grey-bearded man looked closely at the forces arrayed behind me, and he went pale. But only for a moment; the next he was turning his horse, saying over his shoulder, "I do not know who you are, but we will fight to the last breath."

He dug steel greaves into his stallion's sides, and the charger leapt forward, back towards the Protectorate's lines, hooves digging divots in the packed earth of this field that would be filled with the dead and dying before the day was done. We turned back to our own lines, rejoining Urgula.

A horn called from the Protectorate's lines. I rose in my saddle, standing in my stirrups. I raised a hand, and from a dozen places scattered throughout my own lines the deep throated voices of war drums grumbled. More

81

horns responded from the Protectorate's lines, and the main block of infantry moved forward, cavalry repositioning itself behind and to one side. I lowered my hand, and the dead surged behind and past me.

Moargheld stayed by my side, leaving it to Urgula to lead the others, my surrogate company. Moving forward in uneven lines the dead rolled in like the tide towards the Protectorate infantry. The Protectorate infantry set their spears to meet the charge of the dead; Urgula lifted his blade, sweeping it forward from atop his own mount, and the unmounted dead piled onto the spears, not bothering even to hack at them, letting the weight of their bodies pull the spears down.

But the Protectorate infantry did not break. Abandoning their spears and poleaxes a shield wall was raised, short hand axes and sword coming into play alongside mace and javelin. The dead poured forward, dulling the effect of the shield wall by overbearing them.

As the dead poured past Urgula, the dead knight sat atop his mount, watching the carnage with something deadly lurking in his eyes. Moargheld shifted beside me with the two detachments of two hundred each I had held in reserve. "I do not like that one," Moargheld remarked. I said nothing. "I do not trust him."

I grunted non-committedly. "He is mine. He has no choice but to obey."

Moargheld went back to watching the dead knight. "I hope you are right, my friend. But I think I will keep an eye on him, if you do not mind."

"Be my guest."

"As you say."

Urgula waited until the last line of dead came up alongside him before spurring his mount into the fray. The Protectorate infantry were disciplined, and against another enemy, even outnumbered, I had no doubt they might well have prevailed.

But the dead that I had raised were all but impossible to stop, and only by hacking one to pieces could it be even stalled. Javelins stuck out from arms and torsos at awkward angles, and short swords lay abandoned on the ground where the Protectorate infantry had been forced to fall back on dirk as the dead grappled them to the turf.

From the side the Protectorate horse charged, light lances spearing the dead, pinning them to the ground. As a lance struck home, the soldier dropped the polearm and drew a sword or mace, hacking from horseback at the backs of the dead. Slowly, as if waking from a dream, the dead began to turn, and began to defend themselves, to hack at this new threat even as their fellows continued to push back the Protectorate infantry that seemed determined to fight for every foot of ground, paying in blood what could never be bought with honor.

And then, in the middle of the battle Urgula spurred his mount through his own troops, the horse's heavy hooves crushing the skull of one of the dead who was not quick enough or lucky enough. Urgula faced the grey-bearded lord. He lifted his sword in silent salute, ignoring the carnage about him.

The grey-bearded lord paused, then returned the salute with his own blade. Throwing aside his cloak, he crouched over his mount, shield raised. The riders circled each other, Urgula cold, the grey-bearded lord cautious. Swords extended in quick, probing jabs, testing for any sort of weakness that might be exploited.

Finally the grey-bearded lord charged, sweeping his sword in a high arc down on Urgula's head. The dead knight caught the blow on his own blade, tossing it aside with a quick twist of his wrist, then reversing the direction of the blade and cutting into the grey-bearded lord's side. The grey-bearded lord retreated, blood wetting his armor where the blade had penetrated the mail beneath his breastplate. Gritting his teeth he fell back onto the defensive, parrying Urgula's next blow, then another and another.

The dead knight did not stop or pause, merely continued to hammer at the grey-bearded lord mercilessly, refusing to give the old man time or opportunity to launch his own attack, gaining with persistence what he could not with skill now that the grey-bearded lord was ready for him. The old man's wounded side was clearly giving him trouble, and at last the dead knight penetrated the old man's guard again, and then again, and again.

At last, Urgula pulled the tip of his sword back. Flattening his wrist, raising it to his shoulder, he drove the blade into the old man's neck.

The grey-bearded lord slumped in his saddle. His sword fell numbly to the ground, his shield arm lay slack. Urgula paused to retrieve his sword, then ignoring the grey-bearded lord's bodyguard, he contemptuously reined his mount around and headed back towards the main part of the battle without a backward look.

Less than twenty minutes after it had begun, it was over.

Interlude (past)

Freecastle fallen far behind us we marched west across the Tambine plain. Burned farmsteads littered the once fertile expanse of rolling hills and gently wooded copses.

Some, I am sure, had been put to the torch by the demon who would name himself after the domain he had taken at Maorg-mehl's behest, but most had been fired by the petty human barons and counts themselves; the peasants had risen en masse against the wholesale conscription ordered by the King of Chalbine, and when the king had threatened to execute any lord who failed to raise sufficient levies for his cause, the various lordlings had taken to setting "examples" in the hope that the peasants would take the hint. Any that didn't were hung, their wives and daughters taken as camp followers.

We stopped at any intact farmstead we came along; I had run out of food the day before, and though I was not hungry, I knew I *would* be, but so far we had not found enough to feed a babe.

On the second day we came across the remains of a sprawling farm complex in a wide gully cut off from the main road by a swelling in the land. I stopped the company in front of the main building and pointed at four of the dead, indicating that they should follow me.

Part of the roof of the main building had collapsed, but most of it seemed surprisingly intact. We pushed our way into the building.

On the far side of the room a doorway and set of stairs led deeper, presumably into a basement from what I could guess of the layout from the outside of the building. Blackened timbers chipped away, smudging my fingers when I touched them. I decided that the building would already have collapsed if it was going to, and led the four I had selected down the stairs.

There were five of them. None looked to have eaten regularly in a very long time, and the little boy in the center of the circle was the poorest example of humanity I could imagine; sunken eyes and cheeks taut over sallow skin. He could not have been more than four.

The little boy's eyes were haunted in the torchlight as he stared up at me. I felt my stomach rise and had to clamp my jaws to keep the nausea down as my eyes took in the charcoal circle, the candles, the way the others held the little boy down. One of the dead I had brought with me stepped forward, drew his sword.

I turned away, walked back outside with the others. I waited for the one who had stayed behind to return. He made his way up the stairs slowly, walking out into the bitter glare of the sun. He watched me for a moment, then rejoined his comrades, wet blood still on his blade.

Stupid, stupid, *stupid* people. What were you thinking, or were you thinking at all? There is no excuse, *no* excuse for that kind of idiocy. Was it desperation? Fear?

Some things I still don't understand, but one thing I understand all too well is what the priests' hell is like; I know it, because sometimes I feel I have lived it, every day of my life.

13

I put my hands flat on the table and tried again.

"Messir, perhaps I have been unclear. I may still decide to raze the city, if I believe your cooperation to be inadequate."

"Governor," he said stiffly. "You may call me Governor."

"Whatever." I barely held onto my temper.

"Now, as I was saying . . . what was your name again, messir?"

"Aspin, Your Honor."

The governor was nodding. "Yes, yes. Messir Aspin, you must understand my position. How can I be assured that you can control these . . . things at all?"

I stared at him, wondering for the first time if perhaps he was mad. "Would you really like a demonstration, Your Honor? I am sure I can arrange one, if that is what it will take. But do you really want me to?"

"Now, let's not be hasty, Messir Aspin. Surely we can be reasonable, yes? Yes? Good. I am glad to see that you are a reasonable man." The governor dabbed his nose absently before continuing. "There are so few of us left in the world, wouldn't you agree?"

"Assuredly," I replied from between clenched teeth.

"Excellent, excellent. Now, I am sure you understand my position. By your admitted actions, you have put me in a most difficult situation."

I decided that if he repeated himself one more time, I was going to have him strangled as a service to humanity. I forced myself to smile. "Not nearly so difficult a situation as you will find yourself in a moment."

The governor furrowed his brow. "Now, Messir Aspin, there is no cause for this sort of thing, no cause at all, really."

I stood up. "That's it." I turned. "Moargheld, for the sake of the city's populace if nothing else, find me someone who can deal with reality at least marginally better than this overblown pig."

"Of course, Aspin," Moargheld agreed. "Was there

something in particular you wanted me to do with this one?" he asked politely.

"Not really. Just get him out of my sight. Feel free to be as creative as you like."

The governor turned pale. I turned back to him. "Now, *Messir* Governor, are you willing to talk terms with me?"

The governor swallowed. "Aye, messir."

"Good." I looked past him. "You can leave him alone now, Moargheld."

"As you wish," Moargheld said, disappointed. "If you change your mind . . . ?"

"Then I will let you play with him," I assured him. Moargheld nodded, satisfied, and sat back down, arms crossed, watching the governor closely for any sign of further recalcitrance. "Here are the terms I am going to offer you. You have two choices. You can accept them—as I would strongly advise you to do—or you can refuse them. If you refuse them, I will proceed to hang one out of every ten men, starting with you," I told the governor. "If that fails to bring the populace sufficiently into line for my purposes, then I will hang another one-tenth, and I will continue to decimate the population until this is a city of women and children."

"I understand, messir."

"No, I don't think you do," I disagreed. "I intend to hang them for a reason. I would prefer to poison them, actually, but gathering poison in the right form is tedious, and burning them alive would be a waste of good material. What I did to those in my . . . employ I can—and will—do to any who are executed for treason."

"T—treason?" the governor stammered.

"I'm not finished," I cut him off. "I advised you to accept my conditions as much for your own sake as mine. If you cooperate, no one further will be harmed, the city watch may continue to operate, and foreign merchants will be allowed to enter and leave the city after a ten day moratorium on travel outside the city. If you are lucky, it may be that some day the Protector will get around to retaking this city. I wouldn't hold my breath if I were you, but anything can happen. It is, I would point out, better by far than the alternative, wouldn't you agree?"

The governor swallowed. "Aye, messir."

I sat back. "Good. My terms are the following." I ticked off the points on my fingers. "One, all armories in the city will be turned over to the command of my troops, and all weapons other than staves and knives smaller than half a foot will be turned over to be put in the city's armories within a period of three days.

"Two, within a similar period, all registered foreign merchants will report to an officer I will designate who will issue them a pass to leave the city when the moratorium on travel outside the city is ended. Any of the local populace who are found attempting to forge registration in an attempt to leave the city will be summarily executed at the discretion of my designated officer. Three, the youngest child over six of each of the major families will be housed in the governor's compound as surety against organized uprising by the patrician class. All will be cared for and none will be harmed so long as their families do not move against me or mine, or willingly violate any of the terms here set forth. Anyone found to be violating any of the above terms will be summarily executed and subsequently . . . recruited into my employ. For those who violate these terms it will be, I am afraid, a rather long conscription. Am I clear?"

"Perfectly," the governor said, sounding miserable.

"My terms are agreed to, then?"

"They are."

"Good. Now then, wouldn't you think a ball would be appropriate to welcome the peace between you and yours and me and mine?"

"A ball, Messir Aspin?"

"Yes, you know. Music, dancing. That sort of thing. I am sure you are familiar with them. More so than I am, I trust, but it should be just the thing to put the right note on matters, to calm the populace, as well as assuring them that if I receive proper cooperation, there need be no reprisals at all. An ugly word, that, reprisals. I hope there will be no need for further use of either word or deed.

You agree, I hope?"

"Aye, Messir Aspin."

"Good. I am sure there is so much you will need to be going about. I will assign two men to you as an escort, to ensure that you do not become waylaid by ruffians."

I nodded to Moargheld, who stood and led the shaken governor outside. I glanced out the window at the creeping overcast. I didn't like frightening the governor so much. He was an ass, true, though he didn't deserve that, but I would not take it back if I could. Without it, he might well have been tempted to do something rash that would have just gotten people killed to no real purpose. There were times I hated myself, but this was not one of them. It was simply something I had to do. I didn't like it, but the alternative was too appalling for any sane man to contemplate, so I did what I had to do and forgot about it, at least as much as anyone can really forget anything they have done.

Interlude (past)

I stopped the company a few miles south of Marto, leaving them in a vale while I took my horse and galloped a bit aways. I don't know what I was thinking. Maybe I originally had some idea that I could just leave them there, forgotten, until someone stumbled onto them. I just don't know; it was so long ago. I had slowed to a walk, I remember that. My horse brushed its nose over the ground.

Occasionally it would give the grass a tentative nibble, then stop, puzzled. It would have been amusing if it hadn't been so sad. How much worse was living death for an animal than a man, I wondered. Or a woman, for that matter. Habits, it seemed, were very hard to break.

I thought about going home. It would not have been hard. A few days, maybe a week at the most, and I could be back across the Pourtopaine River. Maybe I could even find the riverman who had taken me across the first time. I gave a short, bitter laugh as my horse continued its futile efforts to fulfill its horsey instincts. I couldn't imagine what my mother, what my brother would say.

More importantly, what would—what could I say? No, I couldn't go back. You never can, I suppose.

There, on the ridge in front of me, stood a man. He had a sword, yes, but it was sheathed, so I felt in no immediate danger.

His beard was cropped close, as if by a knife, and his clothing was ragged, worn. Not exactly an enormous threat with he afoot and I still mounted.

"Good day, messir," I said pleasantly.

He gave a nod in return. The wind shifted, and he lifted his head slightly, as if to taste it. Ah. Of course.

"I'm not a demon," I assured him.

"So it seems. Not all of those who serve the Demon are of his kin, though."

"Maybe. If you go back that way a few miles you'll come across a farmstead."

"I have no need for potatoes."

"Apples, actually. They were quite good. But that isn't

91

the point. In the basement you would find a dead child, four years old, I would guess, with four equally dead peasants around him."

I waited for a reaction, but got none. Some people have no sense of humor. I sighed. "They weren't the victims of a suicide pact," I added helpfully.

"I doubt they held still enough for you to trample them, either."

"No," I agreed. "I don't think they would have. I had a friend do it for me. A couple of friends, actually."

"Ah. And your 'friends' are nearby?"

"In a little valley we came across a ways back, yes."

He seemed to consider this. "You say you are no friend of those who serve the Demon."

"Hardly. But that doesn't mean I am your friend, either."

"You do not take it amiss that this spawn of the First World is destroying your motherland?"

I shrugged. "Not really. But then I'm not from around here. Where I'm from, the Duke hasn't reared his ugly head yet."

"And your friends, too—they are not from around here?"

"No, they're from quite a ways away." I meant, of course, that they were from the Third World, not Asperine, but it didn't seem to be the time to clarify my statement. He probably wouldn't have appreciated the joke of it, anyways.

"How many friends do you have?" he said at last.

"Eight hundred, more or less."

His eyes widened. "Eight *hundred*?"

"More or less," I hedged.

"I am wondering if you and your friends might be persuaded to fight with us." He hesitated. "We can pay."

I blinked. *Well, why not?* "I like to know who I'm doing business with, before I promise something like that," I said cautiously.

The man drew himself up proudly. "I am Prince Dektor."

The heir-apparent to the ex-emperor of the Seven

Domains. The rightful claimant to the throne in Báuine. The one everybody thought was dead. Suddenly, I thought of a potential problem.

"There is something I think I should mention . . ."

14

The governor's palace was pretentious, vulgar, and hideously brazen, but I found the chief scribe's office to be more moderate; apparently his excellency did not believe in pampering his servants, but that seemed only reasonable given how much pampering he seemed to require for himself. I had the piles of paperwork removed to the adjoining storeroom and set about making myself at home. There was no way of knowing how long before Baron Sevon of Nerine Domain and his forces would reach Capiné. Despite my bold words earlier to the governor, I was more than a little concerned about what the Protector would do.

I had no illusions about the moratorium on outside travel. At best, it would gain me a few days, and at worst, it would simply stir the Protector's curiosity enough to investigate with his Eyes.

My hope was that even if Baron Sevon took the better part of the month to arrive in Capiné, I would be able to fortify the city enough to discourage an immediate attack; I cared very little what happened afterwards, so long as I was out of it; what happened when Baron Sevon arrived was Baron Sevon's problem, not mine.

With any luck, Baron Sevon would deliver my payment and I would be able to rejoin the company north of Gorsau as I had promised the Sergeant. I laid out a large map of the region I had found in the scribe's office on the single rickety table. Ostensibly I was measuring distances between Capiné and several nearby cities in order to estimate how quickly reinforcements might arrive to take back the city, but I found my mind straying increasingly to measuring the distance between Capiné and a particular point north of Gorsau.

Something caught my eye and I glanced up. "Stop that," I rebuked the young man in front of me.

The young—now suddenly old man's face flickered with surprise, then shifted to that of a young woman. I stood sharply, staring at her. She looked at me curiously. "What is wrong, my friend?"

My heart hammered in my chest and I fought to calm the unbidden surge of emotion that almost drove me from my feet as my knees threatened to buckle beneath me. "Where—when did you see her, the girl?" I managed, my hands shaking.

The woman's features flickered again, this time shifting to those of an older, middle-aged man. The fist around my heart relaxed its grip, and I was able to breath again. Moargheld looked at me curiously. "I do not remember exactly. Somewhere up north."

"Think!" I insisted.

Moargheld pondered the question. "In Báuine, a month before I met you in the Sóage," he said at last. "I saw her at the old Imperial Court."

"You didn't . . . kill her, did you?"

"No," Moargheld shook his head. "It was not necessary. She was just someone I saw. She has a pretty face, does she not?" he remarked.

I sat down. "Yes. She does."

My hands would not stop shaking.

She is alive.

Interlude (past)

Prince Dektor looked grim. "Very well," he said. "I agree to your terms." He sounded as if he had bitten into something sour.

I leaned back. He had not even asked if I knew how to fight. When he had brought me back to his encampment, I knew that he would swallow his rather cloying sense of honor and hire me.

His remaining men were filthy, starved, half of them little better than peasants, though the determination in their eyes made me hesitate to call them mere peasants; they were men, and would fight for what they loved, and strangely, I was moved by what I saw.

Prince Dektor stood and drew his sword. I stepped back, slightly alarmed. Did he mean to kill me after all this? He held the blade pointed at me. "Swear," he ordered. "With your blood, if such as you have any."

Fool.

But there was little I could do, surrounded as I was by his men. As if he had read my mind he shook his head. "No. If you wish to reject our agreement, then you may leave freely. We will not chase you." His expression darkened. "But the next time we meet, I will treat with you as I treat with all those who support the Demon."

I looked at him oddly, wondering whether I could believe him. But in the end, it didn't matter; he was offering me a path, the only path I could see, and my feet were already set upon it. I reached out with one hand, gripping the blade with my fingers.

Still bloody, Prince Dektor sheathed the sword. "Now, there is much planning we need to do." He indicated a crude map drawn in the wet mud. "Here is fallen Colophine, here the Imperial Seat, and here, Cataca. Cataca," he said significantly, "is only a day's march from the Imperial Seat. If we can liberate Cataca, we can raise the population and march upon the Seat. With the Seat taken back, the other provinces will rally, and we will take back that which is ours!" Some of the men nearest him nodded grimly.

I stared at him. Mad as my little sister ever was, and then some. Take back the Imperial Seat, with half the Duke's army sitting there waiting for just some fool like him to attempt exactly that?

I started to refuse, then shrugged. Why not? *My* company was perfectly safe. You can hardly kill something that is already dead. I shrugged. "Okay. What do you want me to do?"

"You," Prince Dektor stated, "are to be my distraction. I need some way to draw the Demon's forces out of Cataca, and preferably the Imperial Seat as well."

I nodded, nonplussed. Perhaps, I thought, he was not quite as stupid as I had first assumed. "You wish me to attack somewhere else?" I suggested.

"Yes. But not a pitched battle. I need you to draw the forces off, not simply engage them. You are to attack Alcine, then pull back as soon as you defeat whatever garrison the Demon has left there. March east, hard. With luck you will be halfway to Talmegor with half the Demon's army at your heels before he realizes that it was all a diversion."

"And what about me?" I pointed out. "I'll have, as you so quaintly put it, half the Duke's army at my heels. I'm not particularly eager to commit suicide, you know?"

Prince Dektor tried to hide the look of contempt that suddenly flashed across his face. "No, it will not be suicide. I would not expect a *mercenary* such as yourself to risk your hide unnecessarily. The Demon has ways of learning of things quickly at far distances; I do not know how as yet, but we know he does. As soon as he realizes that you are a diversion, he will, be sure, order the bulk of whatever force is chasing you to break off and head back to the Imperial Seat in an effort to retake it. You may have to bloody your hands a little, but it should not be anything you cannot take care of."

I nodded again, thoughtfully. "And the payment?"

Prince Dektor looked disgusted, but he answered anyways. "As agreed. Half now, half when we next meet."

"And if your plan fails?" I pressed.

The heir to the fallen empire turned away, but paused

as he did so. "Make sure it does not, messir. Make very sure it does not."

Two of Prince Dektor's followers escorted me to a rise in the hill, and two gunnysacks richer they left me there to return to the company of the dead. The one who had stayed behind at the farmhold to destroy the abomination in the making was waiting for me when I returned. I pulled my mount up in front of him.

"Is there a problem?" I inquired.

For a moment he said nothing. When at last he spoke it was not at all like I had expected; on the contrary, he sounded eerily human. If I closed my eyes, I did not think I would have known him as I did. "You need help."

"Maybe," I answered cautiously.

He nodded.

I took a deep breath. "All right. I need to draw off part of the Duke's forces by attacking Alcine."

He was still for a while. "If you do that, you will be trapped between the sea and the Sóage."

I shook my head. "I think I have that covered. If we can pull the Duke's forces off and evade them for a few days, they will turn around after bigger game."

"Explain."

He waited in silence as I recounted Prince Dektor's plan. "It will not work."

"Maybe."

"The payment. Before or after?"

"Half now, half later. I'm not stupid." I paused. "Do you have a name?"

"Yes."

"Well?"

"Hogennen."

"What kind of a name is that?"

"A nomad's name. There were two brothers. That is what they called me."

"Don't you have a real name? What did your mother call you?" I pressed.

He said nothing.

I sighed, exasperated. "Well, I can't call you something I can barely pronounce." Still he said nothing. "Fine.

98

Sergeant, get the others organized into some sort of marching order, and let's get a move on it. It's a few days to Alcine, and we need to pick up food on the way for me."

The Sergeant moved away towards the other, and again, I was alone.

Eight hundred men walked at my heels, none drawing so much as a breath. The creak of leather and rusted metal mixed in with the wind and the too-loud sound of my own heart beating in my chest as I guided my mount forward, the clumsy clop of the handful of cavalry I had raised gathered about me, dust pulled from a hundred graves, from a thousand, to serve *me*.

Smoke rose behind us, the charred remains of the garrison at Alcine smoldering still. The Duke's chattel had not even bothered to fight, and to say his servants had been badly outnumbered was the understatement of a hundred years. The commander of the garrison was dead, impaled on the Sergeant's own sword. His men had fled, and only the handful of demon bodyguards the Duke had ordered to follow the garrison commander had remained, and when their commander fell his second gestured to the demons and they laid down their weapons in a gesture of surrender.

I had opened my mouth to give the order to conduct them to a place where they might be held when the chamber erupted into violence. There had been six demons, but none of them survived, and none of mine fell despite that more than one bore wounds that would have felled an ordinary man. I turned angrily to the Sergeant, but before I could speak he interrupted me. "A lie can be spoken without the need for giving breath to word."

He looked at the commander's second where he lay, then back at me. "That one intended to kill you when you had turned away."

"How do you *know* that?" I demanded angrily. "He had *put his weapon down!*" I shouted.

The Sergeant, he said nothing.

Two days later we woke one morning with five thousand hounds and men who were not men cresting the

99

hill behind us. Though they were nearly a mile away, the sound of their howls echoed through the valley, and it was then that I knew the meaning of fear, and had begun to doubt what I had done.

At their head rode one on a black horse in blacker armor. Gods, why was it always black? Black, black, black, *black*. An iron sword in his hand (for they, unlike us, cannot bear the touch of unmarred steel) his path chewed great gibbets of soil from the dry earth.

Hounds, blacker than the mount but burning with a mad fire in their veins swept ahead of the main force, rolling to the sides to corral us in. I glanced to the Sergeant, but he had not even turned to look behind him at the host behind.

But the hounds did not attack; they waited, and the horseman rode out alone to our lines. The Sergeant turned to me and said, "You must parlay."

I spoke from between gritted teeth. "Why? What purpose will it serve?" I demanded.

"That is why you must go."

There was nothing I could say to that. I jerked the reins of my own mount sharply to one side, trotting out in front of my host, barely even aware that the Sergeant had followed me out along with four others of the spartan cavalry I had at my pitiful disposal.

The man in armor had stopped as I approached, but he did not pull his helmet off.

"What is your name?" I shouted from twenty paces away, pulling my mount up.

"You may call me Sevon. It is I who commands these filth at my heels."

I glanced uneasily at the Sergeant beside me, then turned back to the demon. "What is it you wish?" I shouted back.

"I wish to eat your heart. But that is not what you needed to ask. Ask instead what it is I must say to you. Ask instead why I am not even now feasting upon your meat, sipping of your blood, roasting your brain, so tender, so tenderly over a fire made from the fat of your women." He fell silent.

I considered this. "All right. What is it you must say to me, Messir Sevon?"

He opened his mouth in a grin, and I saw then that his teeth were sharp, like a meat-eater's. "I am to inform you that the Pretender, the so-called Prince Dektor has failed, and even now sits before His Grace entertaining him. Those who followed him have not been fed since they were captured, and will be starved for ten days more. At that point, they will be instructed to feast upon their commander in the presence of His Grace, to sup of his blood and his marrow. His Grace is kind, however, and will allow them to boil the brain before they must eat it. It should never be said by those who live that His Grace is not a kind and gentle ruler."

I felt nausea creep up my throat. "You will never make men do that."

"So little you know of men. They will do it." The demon who called himself Sevon cocked his head. "They always do."

"What do you want?" I said from between clenched teeth, fighting back the urge to throw up. "Say what you have to say."

"The Pretender, the so-called Prince Dektor, told us that you were but a mercenary, and asked us not to kill you. We have dealt before with such, and it seemed a sensible attitude, after you pay indemnity to His Grace's ministers."

"And what is your reward?"

The demon who called himself Sevon opened his mouth again in the mockery of a grin. "I am to be given this land, Nerine. It will be mine when I have returned with you to the presence of His Grace."

I silently cursed the ground before me, and my eyes strayed then to the ranks behind me that were my own, and the masses of packed men and animals who were, in truth, neither men nor animals. The second half of my payment was never going to be mine, and moreover, it was likely that what I had of the first would be taken in this "indemnity".

But I would have my life.

101

I turned back to the demon who called himself Sevon and twisted my lips around the words. "I will come."

Sevon's army brought me to the Imperial Seat, the mottled array of hellhounds and demons scattered about him as he rode, the heavy musk surrounding them like a dark cloud choking away all of the beauty in this land they had taken for their own.

In the days it took for that army to return with us to the Duke, none of them save their master ate. Twice we stopped at villages, and while Sevon's servants watched hungrily peasants—men and women alike—were brought before him and butchered for him to feed upon. Sevon brought me each time, feeding, I think, as much on the revulsion in my gaze as from the meat before him. I turned away at last, not caring if he would take offense. Sevon merely laughed, telling me I would learn.

When we had reached the last low valley before the vaulting palace that was the Imperial Seat I wondered, then, if there could be anything worse awaiting me than what I had seen. We entered through the ruins of what had been the Seat's gate; torn asunder the heavy doors had been broken in the siege, shattered and thrown from their hinges to rest lifeless upon the floor of the palace they had been built to defend.

But how can one defend a rot that reaches from within to grip the heart and wrench it from its place? For it was not any external force that had felled the Imperial Seat, but one that had rested within. When the lords of the Seven Domains brought their demands to their Emperor, it was a strange man who called himself Maorg-mehl whom represented their interests, and when that one had brought about a common peace, it was Maorg-mehl whom the Emperor took into his service, making him the Master of Commons, the highest rank any commoner might bear. The Emperor was betrayed, but not by the one who called himself Maorg-mehl—that one could never lie—but by his own desire to hear what he wanted to hear and not what was said. The Emperor was found in three pieces when the rot that lay within the Imperial Seat ripened and burst forth. His legs were found in his bed, his torso, the arms ripped from their sockets, the Imperial Bureaucrats found adorning a formerly armless statue in the Emperor's gallery. The Emperor's head was found seated upon the throne, so that all might know the Emperor still ruled, if not quite as he had until then, upon the Imperial Seat.

There is a dark sort of humor there, I suppose, but of the kind that you must laugh at or else go insane.

I was taken to a hall where there lay a pair of murals, unmarred, undisturbed as if they were meant to be taken for some sort of strange trophy. I was left there for hours, tended to by a single human servant, a wasted, broken shell of a human being.

At last, the Duke's minister came into the hall, and I quickly knelt. When raised my head, puzzlement crossed my features, for the scent at my nostrils was not the rotted flowers I had expected, but rather the sickly-sweet musk of a noblewoman's oils and perfumes. I stood slowly, not believing what I saw.

My heart lay stilled in my chest, and for a long moment, I forgot to breathe.

"Lady El," I whispered.

She held herself haughtily, proudly, dressed in the fine silks and brocades of a queen, or perhaps, merely the clothes of a pampered, favorite toy. "You know my name," she replied. "That is good. Servants should always know their master's name."

I looked at her again, and noticed how young she was. Certainly not older than I, and I was only a few years past when I had begun to shave. I saw the arrogant set of her features, and the broken remains of an innocence shattered and broken with only the mercy of the grave remaining untaken. I saw her manner, and I saw something else.

I felt my eyes rest upon the slight swell of her belly, she, barely older than I, and carrying something darker beneath her breast than ever even what I had taken into mine. She saw where my eyes were and slapped me.

"I said nothing, my lady."

103

"Your thoughts betrayed you," she replied. "And your eyes go were none other have dared go. I could have them plucked out if I desired."

"I meant no disrespect."

"You have come to pay us an indemnity."

"Lady El, if I might beg a question of you first?" I asked respectfully.

She drew herself up, the loveliest girl I had ever seen, and she was a girl; I did not think she could be older than sixteen or seventeen. "Say what you have to say, then, messir."

There are some things against which even sanity cannot protect. Curiosity, it seems, stands with these as that company's proudest and bravest member. And stupidest. "How is it that you are here alive, when your father is dead?"

Lady El flushed and drew herself up. "This is my rightful place. He would have denied it to me. My lord has given me what is rightfully mine, and for that I serve him, as all should. I am the Duchess now."

"Your lord," I murmured. "But you are not the Duchess, are you? He has not married you, merely taken you to his bed. Or did you take him to yours, thinking to garner something greater than mere survival?"

I shook my head. "Foolish, foolish girl," I said gently. "And now you are trapped in a dream not of your own devising, and you cannot escape it, can you? His seed swells in your belly, and what it will bring forth no sane person would wish upon our world. Duchess? I think not. Call yourself his concubine, if you would be as true to him as you have not been to yourself. Or perhaps you have, after your own way. Is this what you wanted? Is this how you dreamed it?

"No, you have nothing now, less than nothing. If you survive the birth of the monster you are carrying, I do not think it will be you who walks the dark corridors of your mind, or if it is, it will not be you alone, and the eyes that look out from your head will not look upon things of your choosing, and your tongue will not speak of things you would see spoken of. Your lord, the Duke, he will tire of his plaything soon, and if he does not have you for supper, he will give your mind to one of his servants for its conveyance."

Her nostrils were flaring, and I thought she would call for someone to take me away. Anger and fear fell in a tangled mosaic across the gentle curve of her face. Her hands lay clenched by her sides, and I do not know why she did not then strike me.

Nor, truly, did I know what demon of my own had possessed me to spout such sheer idiocy. I did not know that she could have me executed, but I certainly did not know that she could not. That she did not call for others to take me away to some simpler, if briefer fate let me suspect that her position was closer to my speculations than to her own claims, so proudly uttered in that hall beneath the gaze of warring hundreds.

"Go," she breathed.

"My lady, the indemnity?" I asked politely.

"Go!" she hissed.

I bowed, and left. I wondered how long before the child would be born. I did not think she would live long after it was, if the Duke did not merely grow tired of her before.

15

When I met the Lady El there at the Imperial Seat it would be easy to mistake my words for something they were not, to think that I had gotten over whatever infatuation I had had over the girl. I wish this had been the case, but the truth is a far harder burden, for I had still loved her in my way, and whatever disgust I might have felt was mixed with pity, for I knew then—I *knew*—that she could not possibly survive the birth of the thing she carried beneath her heart. If the birth of the monster did not rip her belly open and leave her lying in a pool of her own blood upon the midwife's table, there was no way the Duke could control his own appetites enough not to eventually consume her.

That he had not already done so forced upon me a grudging respect, though at that time I had not yet met him. For a demon, even one as powerful as he, to resist his instincts for that long spoke of a self-control, a discipline that it was hard for me not to envy. I know a little of the hunger that a demon must fight, and it is not a hard thing to imagine the visions that swim before their eyes in the red haze of craving.

The world casts dark shadows, but what we find it so easy to forget is that we are the light without which the shadows could never be. The true terror is not that the shadows exist, but that it is we who cast them. We are their gods, they our creations, and no god wishes to destroy his children, however terrible they might be and whatever the horrors they inflict upon others.

I stepped into the main hall of the governor's palace curious as to the nature of my reception and the result of my request of the governor. Moargheld and Urgula flanked me, and two of the lesser dead huddled behind them, heavy bladed spears from Capiné's armories in their hands, skirted jackets of mail on their torsos. I stopped as soon as I had crossed the threshold, and waited as the governor made his way over to me, his eyes darting this way and that as he sought to look anywhere but at his new guests. Along the walls, clusters of curious nobles watched us, though few seemed inclined to press too far forward.

"Messir Aspin," the governor sputtered. "I am so glad you could make it."

I executed a neat bow. "And I am glad to have been able to make it." I indicated the nobles with a nod of my head. "I am surprised to see so many here. I am particularly surprised to see so many women. I would have though the nobility of Capiné would have been less than enthusiastic about presenting their daughters to the monster from the north."

The governor refused to look at me, sweat beading on his forehead. "It was necessary to encourage them, it is true, Messir Aspin, but I have done as you instructed. I took the liberty of suggesting that were you unsatisfied with their enthusiasm, it would be the nobles who would be chosen first for any . . . for any examples that you might find it necessary to set."

"Quite all right, excellency. I am glad to see you taking such initiative." I judged it diplomatic not to mention the two dead standing three paces behind him. I was sure it was merely out of the goodness of his own heart that he thought to humor me, and not any feeling of general danger to his own well being.

"Thank you, Messir Aspin. I hope all is to your satisfaction?"

I looked again at the nobles by the walls, then returned to him. "Actually, there is one problem that I can see, excellency."

The governor hesitated, and I shook my head. "I see no dancing, and I hear no music. Surely you brought minstrels."

The governor straightened, turning and crying for the minstrels to start playing. He made his way down the hall, cajoling the nobles to the dance, his pleas echoing through to the rafters.

I hesitated, then turned to Moargheld, touching him on the elbow. "You are old, my friend, and your parent, he was older still."

Moargheld nodded.

"My grandfather told me a story once, but I do not

107

know if it was true," I said, looking over the nobles, the minstrels making their way to one side of the hall, all standing in a line as if waiting for the executioner's sword to fall. "He called him the Rag Man; a dirty, thin old man who dresses in the castoffs that even the poorest burgher would hesitate to wear, and he goes from town to town.

"My grandfather said that his father had seen him once, and his father's brother had claimed to have heard him singing a song of a sea maid who gave her voice in exchange for a pair of legs, but that, I think, might have been just fancy. My grandfather, he said he had heard a rich man say that all the powerful knew of him, and none of them would refuse him anything he asked for fear of what he might do to them. Some, those who would say anything of him at all, said that he was the Sleeping God of the Land, the waking dream of the earth, and that someday the land will wake, and the Rag Man will steal all the children who have not said their prayers to the Fifty True Gods and the Twenty Lords of Light."

My eyes fell among the clustered nobles, the minstrels struggling to maintain a spritely tune. "I wonder if we are all not like that, children, waiting for the Rag Man to snatch us from the shadows."

Moargheld was silent a long time. "Your grandfather was a wise man," Moargheld finally said. "I have never seen this Rag Man, nor have I ever heard of him, but there are things that even the eldest dragons do not understand, and there are secrets that the wisest Seers do not speak of. I think your grandfather was right. This I know, though; there are things that dwell in the shadows, and few of them are friendly to your kind."

I looked at the nobles, the minstrels, the governor, sweating as he looked over at me, hoping for some sign of approval. "But that is the way of the world. I wonder if we would strive half so hard were it not for the very shadows we fear."

Moargheld seemed troubled, but he did not reply, and I left him, walking across the hall.

"You seem troubled, messir. Perhaps the music is not to your taste?"

I looked up. "Your cousins seem less inclined to speak with the monster who has raped your city."

"But you have not, at least not yet. Threatening to do a thing and doing it are two different things. I have a brother, several years my junior, and he threatens to tell our father I have been shirking my lessons when I do not have the cook give him an extra pastry."

"And does he?"

The young woman smiled. "Sometimes," she conceded, "but more often he sees reason and does not. It has been years since I could beat him in a fist fight, but he knows he would have a difficult time explaining my bruises." The smile faded from her lips. "I saw the battle. There it is true you slew men, but they were bearing arms against you. I came to you partly because I find you interesting and would know more about you, and partly too because I intend to spy out your intentions, for none here seem to be sure of them." A brief smile alighted her face again.

"And also, too, because none other would, and I dislike doing as others do."

"I am Aspin. And I am flattered."

She lifted an eyebrow. "And here I thought I heard you say you were Aspin. How odd."

I chuckled. "What may I do for you, Mes . . . ?"

"Soraliangila. I am afraid you have met my father already."

"Your father, Mes Sora? Ah." I paused. "You are the governor's daughter, then?"

"I am indeed. And what *did* you say to him? I have never seen him fawn over anybody, even the Protector's Eyes, this much."

"I attempted to convey the severity of the situation to your father, mes, and to communicate to him the potential consequences of any actions he might take. I regret if this has caused you any discomfort."

"No, just curiosity, though there are those who would argue that that is the crueler discomfort of the two. You keep odd company, for a living man, if you do not mind me saying so, Messir Aspin."

109

"It is a strange world, mes, and sometimes the choices forced upon us are not the choices we would choose for ourselves. This situation was not of my design. I will not claim to be a victim of circumstance, for much of that circumstance was of my own doing,"

Soraliangila reached out and took my elbow. "Come. Let us dance. You can dance, can you not?"

I felt a smile flit across my face. "If not, I will learn so quickly not a one in the hall will ever guess I can not."

"Ah, but I will, messir, I will."

"And will you tell, mes?"

"Only if you do not answer my questions to my satisfaction. A spy must have some measure of success, if the spy is not to be cast aside."

I bowed slightly as we moved towards the center of the hall.

"I shall endeavor to fulfill your every expectation, Mes Sora."

Soraliangila looked at me critically. "We will see." She took my hand and bowed her head over it. "Let them see that the dead can dance, Messir Aspin," she murmured.

I chuckled, my hand lightly on her waist we moved over the floor of the hall like twin ghosts, her steps slow, drifting smoke in airy elegance.
Soraliangila's eyes widened, then narrowed as I followed her steps.

"I think you perhaps exaggerated your inexperience, Aspin."

It was the first time she had said my name alone, and I swallowed a sudden knot in my throat, almost faltering in my step. "It is not so entirely different from what the country folk dance in Asperine, Mes Sora," I said.

"No indeed. You are from Asperine, then? They say you are from beyond the Sóage, you know."

"Asperine is indeed beyond the Sóage, though it has the Seven Domains between it and the Waste." I paused. "You do not care what they will say, to see you dancing so closely with a peasant?"

"A peasant does not raise the dead and stand before them as their lord and master," she replied after a pause.

110

We turned slowly and began to make our way back across the floor, the eyes of nobles and ladies upon us, watching as if waiting for something.

I could feel the governor's gaze upon me, and I could sense his frustration.

"True, Mes Sora. A peasant does much more; he takes the seed and nurtures it as the mother does her babe, he watches over it, and when it is strong and high enough, he cuts it down. A peasant is more god than a king, I think. A king can merely kill, but a peasant can breath life where there were only embers before."

Soraliangila raised her head, looked at me. "Why are you here?" she asked. "Why are you doing this to us?" she asked.

The knot in my chest tightened until it was all that I could do to breathe. "I have no choice. Please believe me." The words fell out of my mouth.

"I want to, but I know what you did at Tona," she whispered.

"Please, I had no choice. You must believe me."

"Tell that to the dead," she said, grip tightening briefly, then loosening. She took a step backwards, looked at me.

The strain poured from my body, and I stood suddenly naked, the eyes of a stranger looking upon a promise and a possibility not considered before. I returned her gaze. "I have," I replied. "I already have."

16

There is a seductive quality in the past. It calls to us in the empty corridors of our hearts, it whispers to us from dreams we cannot escape, but only briefly remember when the cold hard light of day shines upon us. I thought I had loved the Lady El, but in retrospect, it was an infatuation born out of loneliness.

Soraliangila was different. She never said it, but she knew I was no noble, no great lord or king's son, and yet she did not care. She saw me for who I was, and she did not turn away. It was not that she did not see my flaws and faults and sins for what they were, it was that she forgave me them, forgave them without needing to say a word that was not already held in her eyes every time she looked at me. She believed in me, and more, in that I would do what was right when the long winter was past and the spread of flowers swelled the soft breast of the earth to burst anew into a glorious pageant of color and scent.

In the dark passages of my mind I walk upon fields of verdant green. The dead lie buried in the earth beneath me, the worms gnawing at their bones, but the revenants are silent. I lift my head to a soft breeze that plays upon my face, and I see a young woman from Capiné upon the hill.

We hold our own truths inside us, guarded jealously from the fears and insecurities that threaten to seize them and steal them away. Dreams are precious things, and only a fool surrenders them easily, but it is an even greater fool who never surrenders them at all.

The governor's garden blossomed with the promise of spring, cherry trees aching with the weight of their fruit, laden down with their burden, and flowers from a dozen different lands lay carefully planted in neat rows. The garden itself was walled in and small considering the care and effort that had gone into it; I did not think it could have been more than a few dozen feet across, but for all that it seemed a strange sort of island, here in the middle of so much death.

The garden, while technically the governor's, was used more by the ladies of his household than himself. One of his mistresses in particular, I had been told by an over-eager servant, was especially fond of it, and visited it. I had seen her once, at a distance; she was younger than the governor, but by less than I would have thought.

I heard voices near the entrance from the palace, and smiled, rising to me feet from the bench upon which I had been sitting. I stepped towards the cherry tree whose shade I had been taking advantage of, and listened as the voices approached.

"But what is this you must show me now, Lily? Surely it can wait. I have to . . ." Soraliangila stopped midsentence as she saw me standing a faint score paces away from her. The younger woman by her side folded her hands in front of her, and I nodded.

"Thank you, Moargheld. I would like to speak with Mes Sora alone, if you do not mind?"

The younger woman shifted as I watched, and Soraliangila took a step back, startled, hands rising as if to ward off what she saw. Moargheld nodded, just enough for me to see. "Of course, Aspin, I am glad to have been able to help." He turned towards the entrance to the garden, picking his way among the trees back.

Soraliangila watched him go, then turned to me when he had disappeared beyond the foliage. She smoothed her skirts perfunctorily, then straightened.

"You tricked me."

"I did. I apologize for the ruse, but I wished to speak with you, and was unsure if you would come if I requested it."

"My maid is all right?" she asked.

I nodded. "She is fine. In the city trying to find a half-measure of green brocade, I believe."

Soraliangila frowned, puzzled. "Why would she do that?"

"She is just doing what you told her to. I do not think she thought to question you."

Soraliangila opened her mouth, then glanced back the direction Moargheld had come and nodded. "I see. And what was it you wished to speak about, Messir Aspin?"

I came out from under the cherry tree and motioned

to the bench I had been sitting on. "Please, shall we sit?"

She shook her head. "I will stand, I think."

"As you wish. I think I will sit, however."

"If it pleases you."

"Thank you." I hesitated for a moment. "There are some things you should know." She waited, and I cleared my throat.

"There is another army on the way to Capiné, and it is not led by anyone in the Protector's service."

Soraliangila sat down. "I see."

"It is led by Baron Sevon of Nerine Domain of the Seven Domains, now ruled over by the Demon-Duke Maorg-mehl, may his passions damn him to a thousand hells."

I took a deep breath. "I was coerced to take Capiné by way of Tona to establish a beachhead for the Duke's troops to begin an assault upon the rest of the Southern Protectorates."

Soraliangila's face was expressionless, but I could feel the turmoil of her emotions hiding beneath the surface of her voice.

"Why are you telling me this, Aspin?"

"Because I fear what will happen to your family when Baron Sevon arrives. I have dealt with him before, and he is as bad an ally as an enemy. I want you to flee the city with your brother and father. Warn the Protector if you wish. But go."

She looked at me. "You could fight when he comes."

I shook my head emphatically. "It would do no good. Capiné would be doomed even if I did. If Gorsau can be held . . . but maybe not even then. I do not think the Duke will find the taking of the Southern Protectorates easy unless he can find a way to cross the river, and there is such a way at Gorsau. I do not know for certain, but it seems the logical thing for them to do once they have staged their forces at Capiné."

"Why take Capiné at all, then? Why not launch such an attack from Tona? What you say makes no sense."

"I wasn't told this, but I'm pretty sure I know the answer to that. Tona was a small town, no more than a thousand all told, though more than that lay in the graves. Capiné is a city of five times that. Baron Sevon's army will . . . need to feed before they march upon Gorsau."

"They will not spare the women and children, then," Soraliangila said, only a flicker of dread in her voice.

"No. They will not." I hesitated. "Will you go?"

Soraliangila was silent for a time, then she stood. She looked directly at me. "I will stay. My brother will stay. You may fight beside us or against us, but we will not stand idly by and let this baron take even a foot of the Protectorates without a fight."

I stood, took her hands in my own. My stomach knotted up again, but she did not pull away. "Sora. Please. Whether you stay or not, whether I fight or not, Baron Sevon will take Capiné. If you stay, you will die, and I." I stopped, looking away. I took a deep breath before I could look again upon Soraliangila. "If you die," I whispered, "I could never forgive myself. I do not doubt your courage. If you want to fight, fight, but fight where there is some chance of victory. Go to Gorsau, make your stand there! Not here. There is nothing for either of us here."

Soraliangila trembled. "Aspin, I . . ." Something flickered in her eyes, and she looked at me. "And what about you? What will you do, if I go?"

I straightened. "I will stop him. Somehow."

Carefully, she extricated her hands from my grip. Breathing slowly, not looking at me, she stood that way for a long time, not moving. At last she looked up, her eyes meeting mine. "If I leave, will you come to Gorsau when you can?"

It was with my heart that I answered, not my head. "I swear to come to Gorsau to you," I said. "Not even death will stop me."

"Do not say such things. Another, perhaps, but not you."

I bowed my head. "As you wish."

The wind breathed through the trees, a ghostly whisper of a promise that had been made that day in the silence between the words that had been said in that garden. "I will go to Gorsau," she said quietly. "I will tell

115

the Protector's Eyes what I have seen."

"Do so, but whatever else, go quickly, and go soon."

Soraliangila nodded, and left the garden.

I left orders at the gate with Urgula to allow Soraliangila and her brother past, and returned to the office I had appropriated for my use. Moargheld was waiting within. I stopped when I saw the expression on his face.

"What is it?"

"Ships have been sighted, my friend. From the north. The sailors on the docks say it will be a few hours before they can tack into the harbor, but there are many of them."

Something cold went through me. "How many?"

"At least forty, maybe more. Those big galleys they build up at Caubine."

I sat down slowly. "Forty," I repeated. I looked at the doppelganger. "That means at least eight thousand troops, maybe ten."

Moargheld said, "We have time to quit the city, if you think it wise."

"A few hours head start will mean nothing if he has hounds with him, and I cannot see that he will not. Can you run faster than a hound?"

"No, but I can run longer, and so can you."

"Maybe."

"What will we do?"

"For now, wait."

"And later?"

I straightened. "Later, I will have to speak with Baron Sevon. Let us see what his instructions are. If they are what I think they will be, we may have a chance to end this nonsense once and for all, though perhaps not in the way His Grace is expecting."

17

The Southern Protectorates stretch over eight hundred miles on both banks of the Seticau River, not counting the archipelago of Larau and the Far Islands. They consist of some eleven major cities and two dozen smaller cities and towns. The individual cities of the Protectorates are nominally independent, but there are judicial, military and, most importantly, economic ties binding them together.

With the Sóage Waste to the north, a superb means of travel by way of the Seticau River that runs like a belt between most of the cities acting as a perfect corridor to send goods and, when need be, troops, it is little wonder that the Southern Protectorates have lasted as a stable political power as long as they have.

Even the Nomads of the Oatrinnen ith Halanere to the south act more as an energizing influence than a detriment, with the irregular raids erupting out of the grasslands keeping the Protectorates alert, healthy and vibrant.

It is not hard to see why the Duke would want to absorb them into his little empire; while there were individual nobles as rich or richer than any Protectorate merchant in the Seven Domains, there are many more merchants than nobles in any domain, and the total wealth flowing through the Protectorates dwarfs even that of the Seven Domains. And yet despite this, militarily the Protectorates are little threat to anyone around them. The individual cities have their own interests, the most important for most of them being their own prosperity, and war is unreliable for business.

Most military affairs of the Southern Protectorates are carried out under two sets of banners. The first, and nominally most important, is the professional army maintained by the Protector himself in Shaur. In fact, this army is relatively small, kept deliberately so to prevent a Protector from ever becoming tempted to do more than keep the peace of the land.

The second grouping of military forces in the Southern

Protectorates are a collection of mercenary companies and private armies held by individual merchant princes, lords and some of the cities. Few of these number more than a hundred, and almost none would be large enough to match the size of most of the professional mercenary companies in the north, but collectively they far outstrip the manpower of the northern companies, if not in experience, then certainly in numbers and quality of armament. In the north, few mercenaries ever have opportunity to own a full set of mail, but it is not uncommon for the more prosperous companies in the south to be able to outfit their entire company in mail, and, so I have been told one time or another, sometimes in new mail.

The point of this is that while the Southern Protectorates are little threat offensively, defensively they are more than a match for any force the Seven Domains could hope to bring down through the Sóage or through the narrow strip of land between the Pourtopaine River and the Waste. It would seem insane that the Duke would think he could pluck this prize as easily as he had the Seven Domains—and if you think I am making light of twenty years of war be assured I am not; given the strength of the Seven Domains and the Imperial Seat, it is amazing that the Duke, even with the resources at his command, was able to succeed at all.

It makes for an interesting question, then, how the Duke hoped to succeed. The Duke had never been a fool, and yet he showed an astonishing degree of patience for a demon. For *any* demon to be able to focus on a single goal for well over the twenty years it took to conquer the Seven Domains almost asks that the basic assumptions about the nature of the First World be reexamined, so impressive is the accomplishment.

Two possibilities presented themselves to my way of thinking. The first method that could be attempted would be through simple matter of attrition. This was, in fact, what the Duke had done to conquer the Seven Domains, but there were discrepancies that made me doubt that this was in fact what the Duke had in mind. For one, the distance between the Seven Domains and the Southern

Protectorates, while not insurmountable, would make effective communications and regular lines of supply difficult. More importantly, the Southern Protectorates had always been far richer than the Seven Domains, and this, added to the problems produced by the distance, made such an approach unlikely.

This leaves the second possibility, which is some measure of trickery or subtlety. Given the political nature of the Southern Protectorates, this would not be impossible. With disparate cities each with their own private agendas coupled with a fervent desire to avoid war, it would probably not prove impossible to stir up resentment and discord between the cities, possibly even to the point of civil war. If the Protector was weak, this sort of activity could easily fracture the confederacy and plunge it into internal bickering, at which point the Duke could simply pick off the Protectorates one city at a time through a judicious combination of deceit, military power, bribery and intimidation.

I had heard of the current Protector, however, and whatever else could be said of him, weak was most definitely not one of the words that would ever be used to describe him. He was responsible for adding High Hold and Botoco to the lands claimed by the Protectorates, the last being a minor miracle, given the almost legendary loathing Botoco has of its neighbors.

All of this, mind you, without spilling a drop of blood. In point of fact, all reports I had seen indicated that the Protector was universally respected, fair minded, compassionate, firm, and an extremely astute judge of character.

I had a feeling that the Protector was not going to take a liking to what the Duke had in mind for the Southern Protectorates, and I sincerely doubted the nature of this dislike would take the form of harsh language.

I was right.

Rumors ran rampant throughout the city, and despite all that had happened, people lined the quay in curiosity as the first of Baron Sevon's hired galleys swayed clumsily up to the docks of Capiné. I had no particular desire to meet the Baron any sooner than was absolutely necessary, so most of this, you understand, I saw from the respectable distance of the governor's palace's roof.

I had sent Urgula with a detachment of fifty of the dead to meet the Baron and inform him of the basic situation; I had no doubt that this would serve to delay any summons of me by the Baron for at least a few minutes.

"I hate demons," I said to no one in particular.

Moargheld, who stood beside me on the roof, shifted his feet. "An unfortunate feeling for one in your position, my friend."

"Thanks."

"What for?" Moargheld asked curiously.

I sighed. "Never mind."

It took almost an hour for the first group of ships to pull alongside and unload their cargo. The Baron must have been on the first ship to pull onto the quay, for it was considerably less than that when the stench of rotted flowers reached my nostrils. I turned, and examined the thin man standing at the stairwell, two hounds flanking him. A thin trail of drool slid down his cheek, but if he wasn't going to mention it, I sure as hell wasn't going to.

I didn't recognize the individual, but I bowed carefully nonetheless.

"I am Aspin."

The thin man nodded, then motioned for me to follow him, saying nothing. I wasn't actually surprised by my guide's lack of communication; Baron Sevon was no fool, and only a fool would let a demon keep his tongue without a damned good reason, and convenience was certainly not very high up on the list. Moargheld and I followed after the thin man, the two hounds waiting until we were past them before falling in behind us.

My, it seemed the Baron didn't quite trust me for some reason. I wondered why.

Ha.

The Walker led us to the long hall where the governor had held the ball I had requested. As I stepped under the arch leading from hall to stairs the smell of rotted flowers rose like a flood to my nostrils, all but swallowing the smell of blood. I stopped as soon as I had entered the hall. Baron Sevon stood to one side of the center, a largish sack at his feet, a pool of blood seeping out from the sides. Flanking the Baron were two more Walkers, and in front of him stood Urgula, arms folded, eyeless gaze cold.

I bowed cautiously and crossed the distance to the Baron, eyeing the sack, wondering whose blood I was stepping in. "I hope your journey was a pleasant one, Baron."

"It was as pleasant as was expected, Aspin," Baron Sevon replied, my name in his mouth sounding worse than any other curse he might have said had he been man and not demon. He noticed my glance and gestured to Urgula. "Your lieutenant and I have been exchanging words. It seems you thought to let someone leave the city, bearing word to the Protector, she said before she died. Your lieutenant stopped the pair and brought them to me. In return for his diligence in your lapse and at his request, I gave the woman to him and promised him I would not permit you to touch him."

Urgula stood watching me, his stare weighted down with a hate so deep it seemed buried beneath a thousand false pretenses. "No one commands me, worm," he hissed. "Look at your woman, and kiss her now," he mocked. "She has not such a pretty face any longer. I would give you her nose and ears, but I have already fed them to the Baron's puppies."

My breath stopped in my chest, Urgula's words sweeping over me in a cascade of poisoned promises and twisted dreams. I wanted to believe that they lied, but knew they did not, knew that whatever Urgula said, the Baron could not lie to me if he wished it. My eyes fell, and I could not drag them from the sack at the Baron's feet. I watched the blood pool silently beneath it, and I felt something glorious die in me. I learned then, for the first time ever, what it truly meant to hate. If I could have ripped Urgula limb from limb then I would have, but the broken body of the woman I had all but killed would remain dead, and nothing would change.

I raised my eyes to Urgula. "You fool," I said in a low voice. "You stupid, stupid, fool."

"You insignificant little strutting worm," Urgula rasped. "Pissing little peasant, shitting in the fields. You thought to command *me*? You *dared* to command me? And you think you feel pain now, it will be nothing when I am done with you. The Baron..."

"Will not protect you," I interrupted.

Urgula drew back a step. "He . . ."

"Told you what you wanted to hear. Fool," I said again, contempt dripping from my lips. "You do not understand him and his kind, and what you have done now proves it." I stepped up to him, but this time he stayed firm. "I will not send you back to the Third World, Urgula," I whispered. I felt along the connection between us, twisted it, tugged it, weakening it until it was almost about to break. Urgula drew his sword and raised it as if to strike me, still unmoving. He shrieked, the sword clattering to the ground, his body collapsing as the bonds that tied it to the world became too weak to hold the flesh.

But not too weak to hold the spirit.

My anger faded. I could still sense Urgula, but I did not think the others would. Trapped between this world and the Third World, Urgula would wait, wait until my death, and maybe not even then. The wraiths in the Sóage had outlived whatever had raised them, and if it could be done once, it could be done again.

I turned my eyes to the Baron. "And will you now kill me?" I challenged him.

"The Duke made me say I would not kill you. You are not a bad servant, just a disobedient one. Disobedience can be trained out." Baron Sevon did not seem angry. "You have been taught a lesson. Perhaps it will be sufficient."

I lowered myself to the ground in front of Soraliangila's body. I lifted her into my arms, the rough cloth of the sack still wrapped around her. I cradled her there, willing tears that would not come to wash away the memories. "I'm sorry," I whispered. "I'm so sorry."

"And will you raise her, too?" Baron Sevon asked,

curious.

I stiffened, not wanting to reply. *I could. I could bring her back.* Something in me rebelled; not so much that I could not face her mutilated corpse, a walking abomination, but more that I knew it would not be something that could ever bring her joy. I held the Word on my lips, holding it there for a long time, not giving it the breath it needed to make it real. At last, I let her body fall back to the floor, the air still silent of its power.

"Her body is her own."

Baron Sevon said, "You will leave in the morning. I have kept the sailors and captain on of the ships alive so that it can take you to Lipannen. From there, you are to do that little trick you do and ensure that if Protectorate troops come to liberate Capiné or reinforce Gorsau, they will not be from Lipannen, Botoco, or Medennen. Do you understand your orders?"

I rose slowly to my feet, looked straight at him. "I do."

Baron Sevon's gaze pierced me. "And will you follow them?"

But I am not a demon.

"Yes," I said, "I will follow your orders."

I stood before the gathered dead of Tona, the air reeking of death. "Return to Tona. If you wish to dig new graves once there, you may do so. In five days I will sever the bonds that bind us. It should not take you longer than three to get there." I looked out over them, watching for some kind of reaction. There was none.

"You will be free."

On the docks of Capiné we found the ship Sevon had promised me. Without a word her captain took us aboard, the sailors eyeing us with haunted eyes. I wondered what they had seen, taking Baron Sevon's army with them from Nerine Domain. I waited until we were out at sea before I had Moargheld send the captain to me.

The captain licked his lips nervously. "We are going to Lipannen, just as I was told."

"There are new orders. We are to go to Narau."

"But messir, that is two days south of Lipannen!"

"Yes. I know."

"His lordship said . . ."

"I do not care what the Baron said. I am giving you new orders. This ship is sailing to Narau." I stopped meaningfully. "And the moment I and my friend are on Narau's docks, you may set sail to whatever port you wish."

The captain glanced at the city, now falling farther behind us as the ship tacked out of the harbor. He licked his lips again. "All right," he muttered. "All right. You have a deal."

The captain swore to me it would take but three days to reach Narau; on the dawn after the fourth day, the ship slid into the harbor at Narau. Moargheld and I stood on the docks as the captain shouted to his crew, the ship leaving port as quickly as the ship could coax the wind. Moargheld said nothing as the morning waned vaguely on. We walked through the byways of the coastal town, the fisherfolk mingling with the merchants who hawked their wares in the street, insisting that if we did not buy their goods their starving children would curse their names.

The sun was high overhead when Moargheld stopped. "It is time, Aspin."

I nodded and closed my eyes. I clenched my teeth to bite back the bile that rose suddenly in my throat. "It's done."

"Are you all right?" Moargheld asked, concerned.

"I'll live," I said shortly.

"So many do not."

I looked at the doppelganger. He raised his head, and for a moment his features shifted before melting away again.

"No!" I said, my voice strangled.

"You need to remember."

"I cannot. Not now."

"No. But someday."

"Never. Never again."

"You could raise her."

I leaned against the town's well, ignoring the chatter of the women as they washed and drew water. "And what would she be? What would *I* be, Moargheld?"

"Human."

I laughed, but it had a faint, hollow sound to it. "It is too late for that," I said, my voice hoarse. "I am done with demons and women both, and the dead can stay in their graves for all I care."

Moargheld reached out, grabbing my chin with his grip. I tried to draw away, but the doppelganger was stronger than I would ever have guessed. "Look at me," he said, and his features melted. "Remember me," she whispered, and I felt tears pouring down my cheeks.

Moargheld's features melted again as he released me, this time reforming into those of a young man who was now shouting cheerfully at a girl who might have been his sister but for what he was saying. Moargheld watched the man for a moment longer, then turned back to me. "Before he abandoned me, my parent told me something I will never forget. He said, 'Remember. For when we are all gone, it will be in the memories of others that we live.' She lives within you, and she lives in the Third World. If you cannot bring her back, you must let her go, my friend. Let her go."

"Leave me alone."

Moargheld cocked his head. "I do not think you mean that."

"I do mean it. Go away."

"If you will not have it any other way, I will go, my friend. But before I go, consider this. There is supposed to be a man south of here, in the hills, who plays with flesh and the putting of spirits into it. I have visited the Thaumaturges of Boanhogrinbalge, and they are not evil men. If you go to them, maybe they can give you what I cannot." I opened my mouth to tell him that I did not mean what I had said, but the words would not come. I heard Moargheld move away, and when I looked up, he was gone.

I never saw him again.

125

Interlude

I have made mistakes in my life. I look back on what I have done, on what I have been, and I do not always like what I see. If I have learned, I have almost always learned too little too late, and the people who have mattered most to me I have let slip away; not because they had to, but because I did not know how to tell them how I felt.

What I find comfort in is not the silks and rich wines that others do, but in a shadow that extends itself through everything I do. I am repulsed by that which attracts me, but it is only in that attraction that I am able to understand it, and it is only one who can understand an evil thing who can truly conquer it. A soldier who raises his sword in battle for a righteous cause must be able to feel the pain he inflicts if his action is not to be an empty thing shorn of real meaning, for in that feeling of his enemy's pain it becomes impossible to hate.

I wonder sometimes at the desires that flog us onwards. For some, it is a thing we run from; for others, a golden prize awaiting beyond the sunset that we can never quite catch. And for others, the movement itself becomes the addiction, and we cease to move *from* or *to* anything, but move only for the sake of movement. We thrash in the waters of fate, and congratulate ourselves for our victory of having survived.

But we all die, and whether we die forgotten or martyred upon the altar of public honor or private shame means nothing to a universe that cares not what or where we are from nor what we might have done. If there is satisfaction to be obtained in this world, it must be for ourselves, for those who will come after us, or else it means nothing. The universe is not our enemy, but neither is she our friend. The truth is that the universe simply does not care one way or the other, and any truth that we seek to find in it must first be found within ourselves. The truths of the universe are those that we ourselves impress upon it, and the only meaning is that which we give it. The meanings and truths we bring out are not lessoned by this, but made greater for all their solitary splendor.

We are the universe, and the universe is us. It is the seeming paradox that we are most together when we are most alone that lends us our greatness, for it is only when we exist as the trees that we can see the forest, and as the forest that we can see the trees.

When I came to Capiné, I was action without meaning, drive without purpose. In the days that followed Baron Sevon's arrival and my departure, I changed somehow. In Sora's death something else was born in me, and though I was slow to recognize it, it steadily grew until it was a raging flood that I could no more resist than the need to eat and desire for sleep.

18

Narau had once been a fishing town, but the fortunes of trade and politics had let it become something more. When the Southern Protectorates absorbed the Far Islands, trade with the island Tavithnére, a long time trading partner of the Far Islands, was opened. The traditional ports of Capiné and Lipannen began jockeying for control of the profitable trade for Tavithnére salt, obsidian and turquoise, and quickly grew fat off of tariffs raised so high the lord of Tavithnére personally went to Shaur and the Protector to complain. The Protector suggested to the representatives of Capiné and Lipannen that perhaps gouging a would be ally might not be the most polite of gestures, but as it turned out, the Protector was beaten to the punch, his warning (for warning it was) unnecessary.

Merchants from Tavithnére began bringing in shiploads of cargo and dumping them at a tiny Protectorate town a full two days closer by sea that had a more important advantage than its closer proximity; in that town, there was no need to pay the exorbitant tariffs imposed by Capiné and Lipannen. Traders began coming down to tiny Narau instead of Capiné and Lipannen, as the lack of tariffs and lesser distance from Tavithnére meant the Tavithnéren merchant princes could undersell what they had been charging in Capiné and Lipannen and still make a profit.

Trading houses and inns began sprouting in Narau, and within seventeen years, Narau could boast two times the volume of trade of Capiné and Lipannen put together, and if the revenue it gained from the taxes on the trading houses and inns did not make Narau's masters quite as rich as those in Capiné and Lipannen, the city itself did not seem to suffer for it.

Narau's growth had had some unfortunate side effects, however. Unlike Capiné, or even one or two of the larger cities in the Seven Domains, Narau had never had time or opportunity to put in an underground sewage system, so the populace had to make do with a system of open trenches that let the filth flow through at the sluggish pace of cold blood. I kept to the center of the streets as much as possible, but this seemed a popular strategy, and the competition was fierce. I had no obvious weapon, and the thugs hired by the packs by merchant princes from Tavithnére and traders from the inland cities of the Southern Protectorates had little inclination to step aside for a solitary man on foot bearing not so much as a knife.

A beggar asked me for money, and I reached into my belt purse to find only a couple of coppers. I drew them out and frowned. I glanced at the beggar and shrugged, handing them to him. The coins disappeared as suddenly as they had appeared.

I moved on, but the lack of money was a serious concern, and one I was not certain how to handle. I did not have the company with me, so there could be no contracts, but it would take money to buy food and a horse and directions to Boanhogrinbalge. I did not think the Thaumaturges would have what I was looking for, but there was a demon looking for me, and I had no inclination to be where he was apt to find me.

A funeral procession wound its way down the street I was walking, the slow pace measured by the deep voiced bells borne by four priests at the head of the procession, the casket bearing the departed man behind them. I watched from the side of the street until it had almost passed, and stepped out beside a welldressed young man walking behind the procession, eyes squinted in contemplation.

"Messir. I am not from here, and I was wondering if you could tell me whose procession this is."

The young man looked up at me, seemingly unsurprised by my abrupt appearance. "The erstwhile lord of Narau," he replied. "My uncle," he added.

I examined the procession. "It does not seem all that large a procession for so important a person," I said.

The young man sneezed. "Excuse me. Terrible cold. Being lord of Narau doesn't mean all that much, really, though my uncle certainly tried to do what he could, which usually was to try his best to convince Master Merchant Chipotan to stop trying to collect on his gambling debts." I kept pace with him, silently handing him a handkerchief. He took it. "My thanks. Your pardon, messir. I did not catch your name. Mine is Tap Seridius. The sixth, I think it is. It's not something I like to think about."

"Aspin."

"You said you are a foreigner. Tavithnére? Or up north?"

"Up north. Asperine, originally, but most recently of the Seven Domains."

Tap Seridius seemed impressed. "The Seven Domains, really? I heard they have things up there. Demons, or some such." He blew his nose. "Damned terrible cold. Makes my nose itch."

"Something like that."

Tap Seridius sneezed again. "Now, take my uncle, there. A real bastard, if you ask me, but do they say that when they give those silly little speeches at the temple? Not a word of it. It's all about how he was so generous, so kind, so responsible." The young man snorted. "Generous, my foot. He was a miserly old man who kicked his own dog and added insult to the injury of his own compulsive gambling by being a *bad* gambler." He sighed.

"And now it's my turn."

"To gamble?" I inquired.

"To rule. Or at least to make a showing of it." Tap grimaced. "It's not like anything the lord of Narau says really means anything. What isn't determined by the Protector is restricted, administered or constrained under 'advisory guidelines' made by the guilds and merchants' associations twice a year. I get fifty gold florins a year, and in return I'm supposed to look like a dandy and go to Shaur twice a year to kiss the Protector's blind ass."

I looked cautiously around. "It doesn't seem like the people are even paying much attention."

Tap shrugged. "Why should they? The old fart was just a figurehead. He wasn't really a bad man, mind you, but he certainly wasn't a good one either. I really don't think he would have won any popularity contests." Tap paused. "Well, I take that back. The merchants he gambled with, maybe, since he was a fairly good loser, really." Tap examined me. "So tell me the news from up north. How go the affairs of the great and the mighty?"

"Capiné has fallen to an army of the dead, and the Demon-Duke Maorg-Mehl has invaded and is likely marching on Gorsau as we speak," I said.

Tap stared at me, then burst out laughing. He slapped my back. "I like you, Aspin, did you say your name was?" He sneezed, wiping his nose again on his borrowed handkerchief.

"I wish my advisors had a sense of humor like that. It'd make those damn advisory meetings a fair sight more interesting, if not really any more meaningful."

I forced a smile to my lips. "Thank you. I've always been told I was the funny one of my family."

"Brothers? Sisters?"

"One of each."

Tap shook his head. "Me, I've neither. If I did, I wouldn't be in this damnable mess, because I could have ducked the job and dumped it on one of them. If I had a prettier face, maybe Lady Luck would think to kiss me one of these days." He sighed. "I guess there's not much hope for that, is there?"

"Do you want honesty or flattery?"

"Honesty. I get too much of the other from my advisors."

"None."

Tap sneezed, not appearing offended. "Oh well," he said after he had recovered. "I suppose we can't all be gigolos like my uncle."

"Few of us have the stamina, if nothing else."

"True," Tap allowed. "Though there is always pretending. You know, shuttle in four or five girls in a night, and give them orders to appear to be exhausted when they leave."

"I rather think that fools only those with no experience at all," I said slowly.

"Well, maybe, but it does make for amusing sport. Nobody gets hurt, and it gives our younger cousins something to whisper about."

131

I lifted an eyebrow. "And our wives something to roll their eyes about?"

Tap chuckled. "That, too." He looked up as the pace at the head of the line quickened. "Ah, here we go," he said, the gates of the wasting yard approaching. "The old fart will be in his crypt in another half hour at the most, and then I can be back to feeling sorry for myself." He noticed the way I looked at the crypts.

"What, never seen crypts before?"

I glanced at him. "I've seen crypts before, but there aren't any in the Seven Domains. Not in twenty years."

"Oh? Why?"

"Demons eat the dead. Not the long dead, of course, but when they came, it wound up being the only sure way of making sure the body wasn't disturbed."

Tap shuddered. "Grim," he remarked. "My uncle had a Seer here once who talked about that. Rather obsessive about it, actually."

I nodded. "I've heard they can be. There was a schism of some sort a ways back, or so I've been told."

Tap shrugged. "I wouldn't know. Not really the sort of thing that I find all that interesting. I found him rather dull, to be honest." He furrowed his brow curiously. "You like the wasting yard that much? I'm sure it's not my scintillating conversational skills that has kept you this whole way."

I took a step away from him, glancing back. "No, and no. Though it was refreshing, I assure you. I am heading south in a few days, and I need to make some money first. But first I need to establish my credentials."

Tap looked at me blankly.

I smiled, and said the Word, softly, so that he would not hear, and with my mind I reached out and muffled the effect, letting the bodies slumber on in dreamless splendor as I drew the spirits up, out of their places of rest. Around me the air stirred, rippling and contorting as vague shapes and human outlines rose about me, the dust of the wasting yard swirling around, around.

"Who calls me?" a voice whispered. *"Who, who, who?"*

"It is not time yet," another insisted.

132

"They have forgotten me, my children, they have forgotten me!" yet another moaned.

"Silence," I ordered. "I have called you to be witness to these others. When it is done, I will let you go."

Tap had taken a step back, the color vanishing from his face. Around him, others had noticed his reaction and now followed his gaze to see what had startled him so. A tall woman with pursed lips fainted, and the priests arrayed themselves around me, one of them approaching me, his hand held up.

"Who are you?" the priest asked. "You are not a Seer."

"I am not. I follow Nimasgheld's footsteps."

The priest drew back as if slapped. "The Necromancers are no more," he said. "They are gone, their city shattered."

"There is at least one left."

The priest paused. "I would argue the point, but I am ill-disposed to argue with my eyes."

"A wise tact, even among the worst of circumstances."

"Why have you come here?" The priest moved in front of Tap Seridius, the young man still staring at me.

"I am merely passing from one place to another. I have need of certain necessities to continue, and I intended to suggest certain exchanges."

The priest grunted. "You're broke, in other words."

"That is a trifle harsher than I would have put it, but the essence of the description is correct."

The priest straightened, still watching the ghosts hovering about me. "I will vouch for that you can do what you say you can. Dismiss them. Let them sleep."

"As you say." I relaxed my hold, bracing myself as I let the strands of the gathered souls collapse back into the ground. There was a sharp twinge, but little more; it seemed there was something to be said for experience after all. The ghosts faded about me, one of them hovering for a moment longer at the periphery of my vision, then slipping away behind me.

The priest watched me a while longer before speaking. "They will learn of this in Heveith Talige soon, if they do not already know." His tone, his manner were both carefully neutral.

"The Seers, you mean? Yes, I suppose they will. I don't know that they will much like it."

The priest chuckled. "No, they won't. I think they have come to think of the Third World as theirs, too."

"Greedy of them," I remarked.

"Maybe. Greedy of any of us to think we can control what is the resting place of us all."

"Unless, of course, we can," I replied.

The priest acknowledged my remark. "You might still have to argue with certain of the gods about that."

"I'll take that risk, I think. One of them owes me a favor."

The priest lifted an eyebrow, but did not pursue the remark, though I could see he wanted to. "You do not intend to be here long?"

"Only so long to provision myself with a mount and a few days of food."

The priest nodded and turned back to his work, the other three attendants moving in behind him. Tap swore as the priests left earshot, careful to keep his voice low. "By the Land of the Broken Mountain. How did you do that?"

"It's a long story."

"I'll bet. Come, you don't have a place to stay, I take it, if I heard what you and the priest were saying right. You can stay with me, if you'll do me the honor." He managed a surprisingly elegant bow.

"Thank you."

Tap grinned. "I never did much care for the Seers. Damned superior looks and arrogance. I'm glad there's another game in town. Makes for more interesting stakes."

"I thought it was your uncle who was the gambler."

"I may just take it upon myself to learn a few bad habits, if I'm going to be having to put up with same kind of crap that he did."

"So long as I'm not the ante," I said dryly.

"But it would lack half the fun if you were not," Tap replied with a smirk.

I snorted, and followed him out of the wasting yard.

Interlude

As I understand it, there were originally three separate traditions following the use of the Words of Power by mere mortals. The first, largest and oldest of these is said to be that of the Seers of Heveith Talige in Shaur, though I have my doubts as to whether the Seers were truly first, for reasons that should become clear in a while. It is the Seers who have been most aggressive in the indiscriminate pursuit of any and all of the Words of Powers, and what they have acquired they have always guarded jealously.

The Seers of Heveith Talige are governed by the Conclave, a loose association of the most senior Seers called together in congress on a semi-regular basis to discuss those matters that require the attention of the Seers as a whole. Though it has varied in times past, the Conclave during my own lifetime has never numbered fewer than sixty members and never more than ninety-two. Of these, perhaps only a dozen regularly spend any time outside of Shaur, or indeed, even outside of Heveith Talige itself, centered as it is on a small island in the center of the city of Shaur, capital of the Southern Protectorates. Apprentices are always remanded to the custody of their master, and few masters travel, so the majority of apprentices, too, are found only in Shaur. The journeymen, however, are a far different story.

Many of the Seers in the journeyman years never bother to play the infamous politics of the Conclave, and content themselves being advisor to this or that lord. Others serve the interests of this or that member of the Conclave in hopes of winning enough favor to eventually ascend to their number and in the process gain the respect and image of power they desire. Most, however, either insufficiently politically connected or lacking patience with the formalities of the Conclave and Heveith Talige do as their name would indicate; they journey.

Journeying is a formality, and it is not technically required by the Seers, but it is encouraged, in as much as it furthers the purpose of the Seers themselves. For as these journeymen Seers wander, they listen and seek, and what they seek are more of the Words of Power, or versions of them that may be closer to the Pure Forms than those their masters taught them.

A journeyman who comes across one new Word or one significantly purer form of an older, already known Word can gain enough prestige and fame from that one action to become elevated to the Conclave, if not immediately, within a few years of the Word having been proven to the satisfaction of the Conclave.

The stakes are high, and the politics of the Conclave can be even more vicious outside of Heveith Talige than within, for the masters, too, have their own prestige and political power to think of, and while they rarely possess the relentlessness of their journeymen, they have resources and agents far in excess than any lowly journeyman.

Then, too, there are the Dark Seers, who call themselves Summoners now that they have divorced themselves from the authority of the Conclave. It is said they meet upon a rocky knoll twice a year, a place they call Toadebregane Hoge, north and east of the Red Hills on the western flank of the Southern Protectorates. Born in the carnage that was Maorg-mehl's arrival, they have lasted some twenty years, but how many more they will last is something only time will tell, for they are not many, and their enemies are legion.

The second tradition following use of the Words of Power are the Thaumaturges of Boanhogrinbalge in the hills known as the Moare ith Hogennen. They are, in most ways, as different from the Seers as it is possible to be. Where the Seers tend towards excessive aggressiveness and a need for power tempered only by an equal need for knowledge, the Thaumaturges are reclusive to the point of being considered monks by the outside world.

In truth, there is no vow of chastity taken by the Thaumaturges, but it would be difficult to tell the difference from the outside. They live in what any other would call a monastery under conditions even a Seer would call ascetic, though this is not, I think, from any intrinsic desire to strip themselves of worldly pleasures but more because any time spent acquiring the material joys of life would take away from time in their eyes better spent pursuing their art.

And what, the eager young student asks, is the art of the Thaumaturges? The Thaumaturges of Boanhogrinbalge often hide behind the banner of alchemy, and much, it is true, has no small amount to do with that art, but the core of the Thaumaturge's work is the moving and distilling of spirits. Not all—indeed, very few—of these spirits are human, in point of fact. What seems more common for the Thaumaturge to do is to distill and purify the spirits of animal or plant, depositing it at the last in a suitable container. Golems of wood and stone, even metal were their most common receptacles, and while these are rarely possessing of any great intellect, they more than made up for any lack in this area with their strength, fortitude, and obedience. Many are defective or rot away in a score of years or more, and few, unless properly prepared and guided, survive their creators in any useful capacity, but those that do are in sufficient numbers to discourage any outside force from interfering with their studies, and also serve the end of performing many of the physical chores of life that would otherwise need to be performed by human hands.

Unlike the Seers, whose guiding passion is the search for more and purer forms of the Words of Power, the Thaumaturges have only a very few Words of their own, and none at any great level of potency. What they have developed instead is immense patience, attention to detail, and a repertoire of skills that lend themselves to their consuming passion, this being the manipulation of soul and spirit.

The third tradition making use of the Words of Power were, or perhaps I should say are, the Necromancers of the City of the Necromancers. Like the Seers, the Necromancers wore white, but unlike the Seers who all belonged to a single group, the Necromancers split themselves into societies; families of convenience, if you will. Each society was distinguished by a particular animal, and it was a semblance of this animal's skull that a Necromancer would wear as a brooch once he (or she) had been accepted as a full member of the society from their initiateship.

These societies did not represent any strict philosophic differences within the tradition, but rather were an outgrowth of the extended form of the traditional master-apprentice relationship. There was competition between the societies, to be sure, but they were more, I think, a means of establishing personal relationships amidst a larger entity without degenerating these ties to bonds of convenience.

Much of this I know from guesswork, and some from the questioning of those who now dwell in the Third World. Other parts, I know from things I have read or other, stranger sources. Some six hundred years ago, the City of the Necromancers was razed to the ground, those who occupied it rounded up like cattle and put to the torch so that none would ever be tempted to summon up their shades to learn what they knew. All of the Necromancers were thought to have perished; their tradition vanished into oblivion.

Until that day, so long ago now, that I walked in the woods and freed a god bound like a lamb to the earth. Until a god gave me the Word of the Dead, that I, like a fool, grasped as hungrily as a starving man, not understanding the price it would demand of me.

19

I had not, it seemed, needed to prostitute my knowledge for coin after all, at least not in the way I might have imagined. Tap Seridius patted the horse he was loaning me on the rump affectionately. "She's a good horse. Try to treat her well."

"I will." I offered my hand, which he grasped. "Thank you," I said sincerely. "I won't forget this. If you ever need my help . . ."

Tap waved the comment off. "I have reasons of my own. Foremost among them being that I have too little excitement as it is, and I am looking forward to seeing what happens when the Seers realize what you are."

"That isn't the only reason, I'm thinking."

"No," Tap agreed. "I am not so much the fool to see that you could be a valuable ally someday. A small price to pay, a horse and a little food. The food I hardly need, and as for the horse, where am I going to go?" He shrugged deprecatingly.

"A dangerous ally," I warned. "I have many enemies, and from what I have heard from you and that priest of yours, I suspect I may be gaining more I did not know I had."

"A little danger would be preferable to this interminable boredom," Tap remarked. "It can't possibly be worse."

I chuckled. "Tell me that again in five years, and I will believe you then."

"Don't be so sure that I won't." I took the reins of the dun mare and swung into the saddle from the narrow stirrups that had come with the horse. They were awkward to use and different from what I was used to, but I was fairly certain I could handle them without too much trouble, and was certainly not going to complain to my benefactor. "I don't think I will be too long. A few weeks at the outside."

"I'll have a feast waiting upon your return," Tap promised.

I lifted an eyebrow. "So soon after your uncle's death?

Your people will think you insensitive," I said with a smile.

Tap glanced at the stablehands hovering just out of earshot. "And they don't already?" he said dryly.

The major roads from Narau all led north and west towards the other major cities of the Southern Protectorates, but there was nonetheless a road leading south, the direction I wanted to go. Tap Seridius had warned me against straying too far from the road, as the nomads of the Oatrinennen ith Halanere did not consider this land to be owned by any, if not, perhaps, themselves, and though they rarely bothered travellers, it would not be ill-advised to be careful.

The southwards road was dirt and poorly kept for that, but the milestones were in good repair, and as the way snaked along the coast for the first day and a half I could see far out into the sea; though I knew it impossible, I almost thought I could make out the distant shape of Tavithnére to which Narau owed so much of its prosperity.

From where the road turned west away from the sea towards the hills called the Moare ith Hogenennen it took me nearly two days before I saw the hills as anything more than a vague smudge upon the horizon, and even after that it took me yet another day before I was properly in their bosom. I could not have passed more than a half dozen others along the same road as I, and these were pilgrims or tinkers or the occasional herdsman driving sheep to Narau or a wallet full of coin on the backward journey. None of them were any concern of mine.

A late morning sun beat down heavily upon me as I guided Tap Seridius' mare through the thick mud beside a tiny rivulet that was all that was left of what was clearly a much larger stream in wetter times. My mount snorted as the mud churned with her steps, me clinging to her back as her back swayed erratically with her slow progress. The land rose above me in waves of earth and thorn brush, what little progression I had been making tortuously slow and difficult at times even to be sure of, for the swelling of the land made it difficult, if not impossible to tell how far I had come in a day, let alone an hour. It was only by the slowly fading scent of the sea that I knew I was travelling any true distance at all, and it was more than once that I thought even that might simply be a trick of the flirting wind.

A squat, bare chested man was shoveling misshapen lumps of the mud into a wheelbarrow as I crested one rise. He wiped his mouth as he saw me, his eyes watching me closely, though he said nothing. I pulled slightly on Tap Seridius' mare, and the horse stopped, taking a step backwards before I could stop her.

Shifting in the saddle to relieve the aches I felt in thighs I bowed from the saddle. "Good day," I greeted him.

"It is perhaps sufficient for the world's purposes," he replied.

I peered more closely at him, and thought he was older than I had first thought.

"That would be a pleasant thing," I replied. "And an even more pleasant thing would be if you might be able to assist me. I am looking for a man who is said to dwell among those who live at Boanhogrinbalge, among the Thaumaturges."

"What is the name of this man?"

"I know him only by reputation, I am afraid. It has been told to me that he puts spirits back into flesh, as others have put it into stone and wood."

The man straightened slowly, and lifted the arms of the wheelbarrow.

"I will take you to him." I followed my strange companion for a ways in silence, and when I asked him of this or that, he would pretend to be deaf, and not answer. I did not know whether to be offended or chastised, but I do learn, and after a while I shut up.

The monastery at Boanhogrinbalge is more a community, a village, than a single edifice. A few dozen buildings, the largest no bigger than a medium-sized hall, lay in a loose clump in a shallow valley running down from the hills of the Moare ith Hogennen. All were built of stone or rock tightly fitted together without mortar, and without exception every one had the same low, slanting roof made of unpainted heavy wooden planks. I had a feeling they would leak rather badly in the rainy season, but I decided the Thaumaturges undoubtedly had more important things on their mind and were unlikely to fully appreciate any suggestions I might make.

At the head of the valley there stood an odd wooden gate a dozen feet high with a wide crossbeam at its full height, a number of tiny metal charms dancing in the breeze from them. Two stone statues squatted on either side of the gate. My odd companion did not even look at them as we passed, but when I approached one of them shifted, stone grating as it moved to watch me. I watched it curiously, but it did nothing more, and when I had passed all the way through the gate, my companion brought me to one of the buildings, pounding on the door with one fist, his wheelbarrow forgotten in the street.

The door opened, and my companion looked at me and without another word returned to his work, leaving me standing awkwardly in the doorway. "Well," said the young woman, an odd lilt to her impatience. "Come or go as you wish, but do decide on one or the other before too much of the heat escapes. I assume you are here to see my brother. Like the others."

"Others, mes?" I asked quizzically. "I came alone."

"Lugold the Mad," she said. "You are not the first to seek him out. One man even wanted to bring him to Shaur as part of a show to display before the Protector." Her lips twitched in irritation.

"The Protector is blind."

"Of course," she explained patiently, as if to a child." But his advisors have eyes, and many are fond of eccentric sights."

I shook my head. "I wish only to speak with him, mes. Nothing more. If he will not speak with me, I cannot force him."

"One of them said that, as well."

"Did he lie?"

"Only if you count trying to beat me over the head with a kettle when I wasn't looking so he could drag my brother away," she retorted.

I chuckled. "I will come in then, if I may. And I will

promise not to lay a hand upon any kettle, pot or pan in the entire house."

"But you will. I do not like cooking anymore than anyone else. If you wish to speak with my brother, you will cook while you stay here. That is the price."

"Fair enough," I agreed. "It is better than parting with coin I do not have." The woman stepped aside and I entered. The dwelling was neatly kept, if not exactly spotless, and from what I could tell it was a single room with what might have been a loft of some sort above. In the main room across from the hearth was a low stone table, upon it an odd assortment of scattered jars and wooden implements of questionable utility.

Beside it, looking up at me curiously, was a young man perhaps a few years older than the woman who had let me in. His dark hair was only haphazardly combed and his clothing showed signs of having been slept in—for some time, to judge from the heavy smell of unwashed human coming from him. He had most of his teeth, however, and his face was unmarked by pox scars, though he did have a rather odd indentation on his right cheek near his jaw. "Who are you?" he asked.

"You must be Lugold," I said. "I think I have been looking for you."

He smiled. "Well, then. I think you have found me. What can I do for you?"

"You live here alone, the two of you?" I asked curiously as I looked around.

Lugold chuckled. "I and my sister are older than we look, though it is all rather relative. I am still the youngest here save for the pawns. I have rather unorthodox methods, as you probably have heard, but they tolerate me so long as I bring no more than the occasional visitor. You can ignore the sour looks my sister is throwing at you. She feels it her duty to give freely of them—there is nothing personal in it."

I bowed my head. "No insult taken. I am called Aspin."

"And is that your name as well as what you are called?" Lugold quipped.

"For today," I answered. "Though perhaps not for

143

tomorrow. Who can say what the future will bring?"

Lugold's sister snorted, but Lugold himself nodded. "Indeed. Who can say?"

"I have come here seeking your particular kind of knowledge."

"You wish to apprentice yourself?"

I shook my head. "No, messir. I do not. I have some knowledge of a kind and little wish to have more of another kind. What I seek is your expertise on a particular matter."

"A particular matter. What kind of knowledge do you have, then, if not mine?"

"I have some skill at necromancy, messir."

"A dangerous craft," Lugold said.

"It has served me well enough in the past," I said.

"Many things serve us. Many more things do we serve. The trick is in knowing the difference between the two," my host commented.

"I serve no one. No one but myself."

"How sad," Lugold said. "Go on," he encouraged me. "Please."

"I have heard it said you can put spirits into flesh, and make it walk again." I felt myself lean forward, eyes holding his hard in their grasp.

Lugold did appear unduly disturbed. "Of a sort, yes. All Thaumaturges draw spirits out of that which surrounds us, and the moving of them is a natural extension of that work."

"Spirits are not around us, unless they walk as ghosts. There are demons of the First World, and the dead who walk in the Third, but it is only us who claim the Second," I said firmly.

Lugold shook his head. "Oh, no. Not at all." He chuckled. "Excuse me. I have heard that before from Seers, and I should not find it still funny, but it is so very much so. No, Aspin, or whoever you really are, what we call worlds are merely different states. All worlds are one. There is no difference, truly, or we of Boanhogrinbalge could not do what it is we do."

"I do not believe you."

144

Lugold shrugged. "That does not change it. See here," he said, suddenly intent, "you are, even now, drawing air into your lungs. Can you see it? Can you smell it? Can you even, truly, feel it? None of these, but still it is there, still you *know* it is there from the way it enters your lungs and becomes a part of you. Does this mean that the *air* does not exist? No? You see my point, I trust."

Lugold motioned to where a kettle lay on a wood-burning stove. "If I put water in that kettle and boil it, the water becomes steam, it flows out of the kettle and into the air around it, joining with it. Is the water gone? Of course not; it has merely changed its form. You might say that ice is what we look like in the First World, water in the Second, and steam in the Third. Which is true? Which is false?" He shook his head. "You are like the Seers in this. You see only the patterns you have already trained yourself to see. For this you need to look beyond it. There is no true difference. The essence, it is the same. Only the form changes, not the substance."

"Teach me then, if what you say is truly so," I said from between clenched teeth.

"Of course. What is it you wished to know?" Lugold said pleasantly. His sister growled, and he batted away her hand.

"Can you bring the dead back to life? If not in their own body, than in another?" The words spilled out of me, taking shape of their own.

"Of a sort. But I cannot make flesh live again, or move much beyond its death. Sometimes one comes to my attention who has entered a vegetative state. When such a one does, I am sometimes able to instill within it a spirit I have acquired from elsewhere."

"Where do you get the spirit?"

Lugold shrugged. "Plants, usually. Sometimes animals. Never a human. There are some places I do not wish to go. Not yet. They call me the Mad, but that is only because they do not understand what I do, would not dare if they did. But I am not, as yet, mad. Someday, no doubt, but for the meantime I am quite sane, and a sane man has little wish to tamper with things as intelligent as myself."

145

The Thaumaturge allowed himself a slight smile. "Lugold the Mad I may be, but Lugold the Fool I am not. Caution is the wisest of all courses."

I sat still for a long time, not knowing how to answer.

Lugold looked at me quizzically. "What, I take it that you wish me to bring that spirit hovering around you back into its body, or some other?" he asked politely.

I stiffened. A rush of cold ran down to my feet. "What are you talking about?" I breathed.

"I assumed you knew," Lugold replied. "Being who say you are. Unless you are not. But yes, I see you know what I say is so, though you did not know it, perhaps, until I said it."

I felt cautiously with my mind, along the link that bound me to everything I had touched. Carefully, quietly, so as not to disturb the fragile string that he must have seen. My breath caught in my throat as I found what I sought, and I felt the blood drain out of my face. "I did not summon her. I could not have."

Lugold looked interested. "Really? Then either your memory is failing you, or something else has happened. I have heard stories of revenants. Perhaps this ghost of yours is one such."

"She. Her name was . . . is Sora." I swallowed. "Can she hear me?" I asked in a strangled whisper.

"I would imagine so," Lugold replied. "You should know more about it than I, however."

My wits failed me. I could not have called her.

Could I?

I had mouthed the Word over her body, felt it through my bones, but I had not given it form. Or so I had thought. Could she be there, trapped by my own stupidity, my own pride? I had thought to come to Boanhogrinbalge, I had wanted Lugold to tell me what I had wanted to hear; that there was nothing I or anyone else could have done, that she was well and truly dead and gone, and that it was a better thing to let her lie in peace, to forget her in time, if I could.

Now, I knew that she did not lie in peace, that I—or perhaps she—had kept her here, locked her away from

146

that path followed by every man, every woman, ever child who goes to that cold darkness beyond grave and pyre, when the ashes have smoldered and then died and the toiled earth rests silent beneath us.

But it is rare that the universe gives us what we want. More often it merely gives us what we need, and leaves it to our own will to stand or fall, for it does not care which if we will not.

I stood, unable to focus my eyes. "Forgive me, but I think I need to be alone. I will be back in a bit." I bowed and walked unsteadily out of the house, Lugold and his sister behind me, the one chuckling, the other grumbling. The sun ached high in the noontime sky, the small community come softly alive with the sounds of activity, most of them unfamiliar to me. I made my way through the settlement until I at last came to the gates.

The two stone creatures who had been there when I had arrived still stood silent sentry there. Neither moved as I approached, then stopped, facing them. "If I leave, will you bar my way should I return?" I asked. One of the stone creatures moved ponderously, heavy stone head rising to consider me in my stained black cloak and mud stained boots. It did not speak, but I thought it might have nodded, so I bowed formally, and walked past the guardians.

The land around and above Boanhogrinbalge is not called what it is for nothing—Land of Stone, it is an apt name, for little there is not stone of one kind or another, though most is of granite, pursed closely in rivulets here and there, flowing down from the heights to the muddy flats below Boanhogrinbalge. There is some wood on those hills, but less than I might have supposed to hear the folk talk of the wooden men of Boanhogrinbalge, but it was, after all, true that I saw very little of the hills, and it might well be there were forests hidden from my view in the deep clefts and ravines of the place.

I walked until I could no longer hear the sounds of the settlement, the sun above burning wanly above in a vain attempt to warm an air chilled for more than mere lack of warmth shed by an unwilling sun. On a knoll I sat, arms

147

wrapping around myself as I sat there, listening, trying not to hear what I knew I would.

I do not think I could have been there for very long, but it seemed hours that I had sat there when I heard the wind stir beside me, and a voice, whispering my name. I closed my eyes tightly, willing it to go away, to be a delusion of a fevered imagination.

"Aspin."

"No, it can't be," I breathed. "I did not call you. I didn't."

"I am dead, aren't I?" The voice sounded wistful. "Aspin, I thought there would be so much time, but there is none, none, none. The time is sand spent in the hourglass, and now you are alone, and I am alone. But it is the others who will suffer. They have not been warned, have they?"

"Sora . . ." I mumbled, eyes still shut. "Why have you come here?"

The wind tugged at my sleeve, and I pulled my arms tighter about me. "I have come here because this is where you are. I wanted to be with you, Aspin. I thought you wanted me with you, as well."

"You are dead! Leave me!"

"I am not Moargheld, to be dismissed so. I do not serve you, not out of duty or guilt. You must warn them. I could not. I remember. . .I do not know what I remember. Pain, and something else. But I cannot remember having left Capiné, so I do not think I ever saw Gorsau. I did not, did I?"

"No, you did not," I said, the words coming out in a strangled whisper. "You were killed, and it was my fault."

"You could not have killed me."

"Sora, you said you did not remember. You cannot know that. You cannot know what happened."

"But I do. I do not remember, but I know that you would not kill me or cause me harm. I am sure of this, or I could not be here."

"I. . .Sora, I came here because I thought I might be able to bring you back, after a fashion. In living flesh. I heard that there was one here who had done such, and I

148

thought maybe he might do this thing for me. But now I am not sure, I do not know if it can be done. I will try, if you want me to." I opened my eyes, strained

in the harsh light of the afternoon sun to see the shifting in the air, the curve of the wind that might be a woman's lip.

"Aspin, you must tell them, you must send them word," the voice urged. "Before it is too late. They will not know to reinforce Gorsau, and thousands more will fall, and not just my poor Capiné."

"I am afraid, Sora."

"We are together, my love. Fear no more, for I will be with you, and none but you can send me away."

I lifted my face. "Is that what you want me to do?" I asked.

"I want . . ." the wind died slowly, and a sad sigh faded into the air.

I listened for a long time, but there was only silence, and if the wind muttered wisdom it was in no language I could understand.

Interlude

There are those who will say I cannot have loved her for all that I knew her only a few short days. In truth, I think it was not so much what there was between us that I grieved for, but what could have been. There was a strength in her I could recognize from the first moment I saw her, from the courage it must have taken her to approach me when no other would, from a million other things that the eye sees but the mind does not record.

Soraliangila did not tell me what I wanted to hear, but what I needed to hear, and that, had there been nothing else, would have drawn me to her. What is love, after all, but a recognition of possibilities, a recognition of what might be coupled with a fear that it might not, that the bud will remain a bud, never knowing the touch of the sun upon petals spread wide. She opened my eyes to truths I had known but refused to face, to a truth that I had been hiding, afraid of what I might see should I open my mind as another might open their eyes.

We protect innocence, but we should never nurture it. A child's innocence we delight in, but the innocence of a man full grown is a thing to be ashamed of. We are meant to grow, to understand, to become in the fullness of time the course of our lives. The innocence of a child reminds us of a time when the world was new, when we did not know the things that people can do. But which is the greater glory, to stay in the womb of ignorance, or to emerge from it into the day, ready to fight for a world that will have been made better for our presence when we are gone, whether it be with words or cunning or steel?

20

"I want your help," I stated.

Lugold watched me, face unmoved. "Why?"

"You have armies here, armies as great as any I might raise. There is a rot in the Seven Domains, and now it threatens to spread to the Southern Protectorates, to Asperine, to Tavithnére. Even now, it spreads. Tona is fallen, and Capiné. Gorsau will be next, and after that it will spread throughout the southlands."

The Thaumaturge chuckled. "I am not a warlord, and I am not, in truth, even a friend of yours. Our duty is to study, to learn. Not to fight. We would lose something greater than mere blood were we to go with you, and we will not."

"If you do not fight, Maorg-mehl may smother us all. Is that what you want?"

Lugold leaned back. "Of course not. Do not be absurd. But we are scholars, not soldiers. I doubt we could help you if we wanted. There are not many of us."

"There is only one of me," I said from between clenched teeth.

Lugold shook his head, chuckling, and his sister snorted.

"Arrogance and pride make poor lovers."

"And I would be the greater fool were I to ignore what I have," I shot back, suddenly furious. "If I had nothing more than my fingernails, I would fight the same. Do I have power? Yes! But I would be more arrogant still were I to wallow in the pride of sanctimony."

"Violence serves only itself," Lugold retorted.

"And you, how well do you serve, you who stand back and let the butchers of the world do their will upon it?" I straightened, and my voice became low. "Yours is the arrogance, yours is the pride. If you will not fight, at least I will, and if that damns me to oblivion or a hundred hells, then so be it. I accept that price, if it will mean the deliverance from the madness that spreads through the north."

Lugold looked at me sadly. "Do you hate them so

151

much?"

I straightened. "No. I do not hate them. But neither will I bed down with a mad dog. I do not seek revenge. Merely sanity." I bowed. "I thank you for your hospitality. Your name will receive no blemish from my lips." I turned and left, the door clattering shut behind me.

I took my time gathering Tap Seridius' borrowed mare, giving my anger the space it needed to settle. At last I could delay no longer, and I swung into the saddle and rode towards the gate. A few men and middle-aged women watched me as I left, but I kept my eyes forward, not wanting to meet their gazes. *I am a fool. I should never have come here.*

I pulled up on the reins sharply when I saw who waited by the gate. "You. What do you want?"

Lugold the Mad's sister waited there, crouched beside one of the stone gargoyles. As she heard me she petted it once like a favorite dog and brushed her lap, standing. She looked at me with narrowed eyes. "There is no honor in what you do, you know," she said. "Only death can come of it."

"Life begets death as surely as death begets life," I said quietly. "I do not think it is ever otherwise."

"You love death!" she said, anger creeping into her voice.

"Is that it? She is your lover, you her slave. Well, if you would sew the ground with blood, does it ever occur to you that that is all you can ever reap?"

The mare shifted uneasily beneath me. I shook my head.

"No. I do not love death." I looked more closely at Lugold's sister. "But neither do I hate it." I tapped the reins on the mare, and left through the gates.

Interlude (past)

When does a story end, and where does it begin? Maorg-mehl, called Duke of the Seven Domains, had taken twenty years to subdue the domains. Twenty years where men fought men as much as they ever fought demons. Mercenary companies fought for whichever side promised the most coin or the best chance for loot, never caring at the consequences, never dreaming what those consequences might be.

By the time I crossed over the Pourtopaine River into the Seven Domains the wars were all but over, the mercenary companies slaughtered to the last men or else fled into the south. The Iron Men, Veldane's Hammer, the Band of the Blue River went south across the Sóage or east across the sea, fleeing a master who knew nothing but hunger, and needed only to feed. They were the lucky ones, though none of those survived with more than a tenth of the men they had once had.

Thousands died, and yet it was only after when the Duke called the children out of the towns and villages, and the people feared, but dared do nothing. Maorg-mehl's servants reassured them, they told the burghers and village smiths and weavers that their children would not be harmed, that their children would be safer even than those who were their parents, locked tight behind the walls of their cities. The Seers told the people that a demon could not lie, and so the people waited, and prayed to the Fifty True Gods and the Twenty Lords of Light.

In time, the Duke's servants brought the young ones back.

And the children, they hungered.

21

It had taken me nearly four days to cross between Narau on the coast of the sea, and Boanhogrinbalge in the lap of the Moare ith Hogennen, but it took me only three to return. Unlike the gated north wall, the old southern wall of Narau had long since crumbled, and it was clear that over the years the disrepair had been accelerated by the cannibalizing of the stone from the walls for townhouses and hovels alike. Where the northern border of Narau was sharply kept and strictly delineated, the southern seemed little more than a skirt of buildings, roughly laid streets and roads winding their way between the dyers and warehouses and the smaller dwellings of the fisherfolk who worked on the boats of the rich that trawled the deep Ocean of Stars.

Tap Seridius' mare was a good animal with the markings of the noble caste of the Southern Protectorates, but such were common enough that their only effect was to cause a small part in front of me and a larger wake behind me as I moved through the crowds, waiting until I was in a better part of town before dismounting.

A guard stopped me as I stopped at the fountain where Moargheld had abandoned me. I held the mare's reins, letting her drink her fill, and the heavy-chested man put his hand roughly on my shoulder.

"Where did you get that horse?" he demanded.

I turned to face him. "She was a gift," I replied. "And I think you had better remove your hand."

The guard tightened his grip on my shoulder. "Or you will break it?" He laughed, and it was an ugly sound. "I do not think so. In Capiné they cut off the right hand of those who steal. Here we do worse. Tell me where you got the horse, and maybe I will argue for leniency for you."

"No," I said softly. "But there are other things I can do that I do not think you will like. It will go easier for you if you do as I say. I have no wish to prove my point, certainly not over an idiotic point like this. Truly, the horse was a gift, from your own lord."

The guard grimaced. "Little Tap. He is no more lord

of this city than I."

"So he said," I agreed amiably. "But then, the horse was his to give, and give her to me he did, so that is between he and I, leaving you quite out of the picture. If you do not wish to believe me, you are welcome to accompany me to the palace to ask him, for that is where I intend to go as soon as my mare drinks her fill."

The guard released my shoulder, and I had to restrain the impulse to rub it; he was a full head taller than I, and his grip was, shall we say, slightly stronger than mine. The guard looked sour, and I will not repeat what he said then since it has little to do with anything other than my own ancestry; and truly, I know for a fact that the horses had stayed in the pasture at night, even in the wettest weather.

I chuckled to myself, as much to annoy the guard as to express any real amusement I might have felt. I dawdled over watering the mare, enjoying watching the guard fidget. At last I could think of no more excuses, so I took the reins in my hand and led horse and guard towards the palace.

It took some time to get into the palace, and even longer to convince a rather dubious page to summon Lord Tap Seridius. I had been waiting for only a few minutes when Tap barreled down the stairs two at a time, somehow managing not to trip on the long cape he wore trailing behind him.

"Aspin!" Tap cried. He frowned at the guard beside me. "Who's he?"

I glanced dryly at my escort, then turned back to Tap. "I think it would have perhaps been wiser to just give me enough money to buy a horse at the market than to give me one out of your own stables."

Tap looked confused for a moment, then burst out laughing. "You know, I hadn't really thought about that, but I do think you are right," he remarked. He waved away the guard. "I did indeed give him the horse. You can go now."

The guard looked darkly at his lord and bowed coldly. "As you wish." He turned and left, his step deliberately heavy. When the guard had slammed the door shut, a shadow fell over Tap's face.

"I thought you were joking, Aspin," Tap said uneasily.

"What do you mean?"

Tap shook his head. "Capiné. The monsters from the north. I received a message two days after you left from the Protector instructing me to bring as many men as I could muster to Medennen, where they are to be put under the control of Warlord Gotib Sos. I will remain nominally in command, of course, but that's all a polite fiction, and the Protector was not very gentle about salving my pride." Tap did not seem upset, and the lines about his face seemed more worried than resentful.

"Then he knows," I said, relief flowing through me.

"That the monsters have taken Capiné? Yes. I believe he intends to ferry troops across the southern delta and march more down from Gorsau, but I am only guessing that from his orders."

Tap paused, and his next words he spoke with deliberation. "I am certain he does not mean to wait for the monsters to attack again. He intends to take the battle to this foreign duke."

"A brave gesture, but it could get us all killed."

Tap looked at me curiously. "Eh? How so?"

"Oh, certainly, in another situation, facing a human army, it would not be so bad a move. I am betting there are political motives to this as well as not wishing to give time for the Duke to consolidate his hold on Capiné. The Seers should know better, though. The longer the Protector can wait, the weaker the Duke's forces will become as they slaughter the rest of the population. Doesn't he listen to his Seers?"

Tap paled. "Slaughter the rest of the population? The Protector cannot permit that!"

I forced my voice to a hardness I did not entirely feel. "To save the Southern Protectorates, it may be necessary to sacrifice Capiné." I felt sick to my stomach. "No, even that is too kind. It *will* be necessary. There is nothing worth saving in Capiné by now, or at least nothing that could be saved by the time any army the Protector could send reached Capiné."

"What do we do?" Tap said in a small voice.

"We do as the Protector bade you," I said sharply. "You raise as many men as you can find weapons for, and march them to Medennen. In the meantime, you will send two other messages."

"Two?"

I nodded. I held up a finger. "One, you will send a message to the Protector in Shaur, urging him in the strongest possible terms to send the armies to Gorsau, and *not* to attack Capiné."

"He will not listen to *me*!" Tap exclaimed.

"He will," I said grimly. "Because you will tell him that a ship captain docked yesterday and came immediately to you, informing you that the Duke's army has already begun marching."

"But that's a lie!" Tap protested weakly.

"Yes. It is. Do you care more for the truth, or to save your people?"

Tap swallowed. "You said two messages?"

"Correct. The second message is to be taken by fast courier to Gorsau, and north and west. The Protectorate has allies it does not know it has, but they must be told where to go."

"Allies?"

"Allies," I said firmly. "Now, when did the Protector want you in Medennen by?"

"Five days. I intended to issue the order to march tomorrow morning."

I shook my head. "Make it tonight," I said. "It will take them until morning just to get the logistics handled, and if you wait until the morrow, you will waste most of the morning and be lucky to begin marching by late afternoon."

"The guilds are threatening to withhold their support if we try to conscript any guildsmen," Tap warned.

"You are lord," I said bluntly. "Maybe it's time you started acting like one."

Tap straightened. "You're right. You're absolutely right." His expression darkened. "They won't like it."

"Only fools and old men look forward to war," I said. "But still we go."

Tap sent for a scribe and a page; the page he sent to

157

fetch a courier and the Master of Pigeons, the scribe he had take down a message to send to the Protector. When he had finished he called for one of his advisors and had the old man ambling out a moment later, the order for marching in one hand, an order for conscription of the guildsmen in the other. Even so, it was not until an hour before noon the next day that the first elements of Tap's conscripted army and tiny band of regulars left Narau's northern gate on the road to Medennen; another detachment were sailing in by ship, but Tap's own coffers were not nearly as full as those of the guilds', and he did not have enough money to hire the captains necessary to send the whole force by sea.

"Who are these allies?" Tap asked as we rode between two of the makeshift companies on the northern road. "You didn't say."

"Use your imagination. You know what I do."

"The dead?" Tap suggested. "I mean, they can really fight? And kill?"

"They can fight," I replied. "And yes, they can kill."

"Do you have a lot of them?"

"Quite."

Tap cocked his head. "What's bothering you, Aspin? You haven't so much as asked for the bathwater today."

I looked away from him, northwards towards the river and the Seven Domains far beyond them. "I'm not sure we can win this one."

"Why not?"

I glanced back at him. "I've seen what they do. This will not be easy."

"But you've beaten them, haven't you?"

"Never this many. Never a whole army. I am not really certain your men will be able to do any real damage to the Duke's. We may well die without even having done any serious damage to the Duke's host."

Tap was silent for a long time. "Why are you doing this, Aspin? Helping us, I mean. This isn't your country. It isn't your fight. Things are going to get ugly pretty soon, and you know as well as I do that no matter where you are in the lines, if things go badly, you may fall."

158

"Some things are better left unanswered." I held up my hand as Tap opened his mouth. "Leave it be, Tap. Please. I won't tell you, and you aren't going to pry it out of me, so don't even try."

"All right. Be that way." Tap whipped the reins of his stallion on the horse's withers and trotted off in a huff.

I sighed.

22

Politics make for strange bedfellows in the sanest of places, and rarely do they make stranger bedfellows than in the Southern Protectorates.

I don't think anyone really knows how the system existing in the Southern Protectorates when I entered its borders came to be, and if you are foolish enough to ask the legates or philosophers, each will give a different answer from the one before, and *none* of them will admit to not actually knowing. If this sounds odd, be assured; there are far stranger things in the Southern Protectorates.

The position of the Protector is not a hereditary one. It is potentially one of the most powerful seats in the world, yet it demands in turn the harshest price. Those who seek power by the traditional avenues are reluctant to pay its prices, and generally content themselves with power of another nature, that over one or another of the individual cities that make up the Protectorates, each governed in its own way.

The one who would be Protector is called forth by duty, not love of power, and the means used to assure this are devious, if ruthless. Once approved, yet before actually assuming power, the new would-be Protector is stripped naked before the populace, and there, in front of the world, is ripped clean of arrogance. He formally renounces any ties that might have bound him before—no promise, no oath, no familial or romantic tie is supposed to be retained. His eyes are plucked out, so that he must rely on those around him for his power, for the Protector must be as much the servant of the state as the state is his servant. He is castrated and branded upon thigh and arm, and put before the people to serve them.

And then he is named to the most powerful position in the known world.

At his behest the Protector has several tools at his disposal. The first of his tools, and most prosaic, is the bureaucracy, but it is arguably the most powerful. The second of his tools are his Dragons. His Dragons are bodyguards, but not normal men and women, but rather something more, and something less. Through means of some ritual known only to the Seers, those who will become a Dragon step into the Fire at Heveith Talige and come out purified and, except in rare cases when the choice was made for the wrong reasons, unburned. The Dragon is still mortal, but can change his or her shape into that of one of the great dragons, thirty feet of serpentine glory, scales gleaming red for the sun and the fire that waits at the end of the world. The change is not without its price, but they make for bodyguards that the rest of the world might envy.

The third tool at the Protector's disposal are his Eyes. It is axiomatic that none but the Protector knows who they are, though this is not quite true, for there are a few who are known for what they are. The Eyes are spies, watchers, advisors. They listen, they watch, and they tell only the Protector what they see. The fourth tool are his Hands. The counterpart to the Protector's Eyes, the Hands are known to all, for each and every one has been branded with the mark of a hand on the left side of their faces. Couriers, assassins, executioners, jailors, diplomats and a hundred other secret things, they give up even their name when they enter the service of the Protector. They are utterly loyal to the Protector, and are said to be incorruptible.

And then there are the Seers, though they cannot truly be said to serve the Protector at all, but rather are more in the way of his allies, and some would say that they play a game all their own, and in that game, the Protector and all the Protectorates are nothing more than a pawn to be pushed about some great board.

Medennen stood on the southern shores of the Seticau River, one of that common breed of settlements here in the south where there seemed always to be more merchants than laborers. Barges crowded the docks on the east side of the city by the river where we waited the arrival of the last of Narau's conscripted troops. The dockworkers were all of a kind, heavy, slow-fisted men who would as soon break your nose as give you directions to the nearest privy, but there was a fear in their eyes. Not

161

from the rumors of demons; these men had heard—and spread—stories of worse than Maorg-mehl's brood in their time. What they feared was something more elemental to them, for as they watched the sullen faces of the conscripts marching off the barges ferrying in the troops from farther east they could easily see themselves soon in a similar position. The Protector was not liable to overlook them, and conscription was not noted for paying well.

The mere fact of the conscription was enough to worry even the steadiest of the traders who had flocked into the city, for the Southern Protectors relied almost exclusively on the services of paid mercenaries. For the Protector to call for conscription spoke of a threat to the very underlying integrity of the Protectorates, and few of the merchants were slow to realize this. Medennen was a popular haven for the multitude of small independent mercenary companies of the south, and the empty taverns more even than the abandoned bathhouses revealed the uncomfortable fact that the city was empty of mercenaries.

We were in Medennen for less than a day; by nightfall Narau's troops were already being loaded on to the barges again to be ferried upriver to Gorsau. It would take most of the barges two trips, and some three, and from the word on the docks, conscripts and soldiers from Lipannen had come through two days ago. If rumor could be believed, there were close to fifty thousand men under arms at Gorsau already, and before the week was over there would be close to sixty. They would outnumber Baron Sevon's army by a considerable amount, and, further, the baron would be handicapped by the loss of my undead.

By now there was no doubt that Sevon knew of my treachery, and the only question in my mind was what he would do about it. He might send another assassin after me, as he had Moargheld, but for him the situation would be getting critical, and the baron was unlikely to want to rush any revenge. More likely he would simply wait until Gorsau was in ashes, and then take his time.

This did not exactly comfort me.

It took us a day and a half to reach Gorsau from

Medennen by barge, and by the end of it I was pale and retching to the considerable amusement of Tap and the bargemen. A barge, it seems, is not like a ship. Ships have a certain mass, and though it is true they do rock, there is a certain grand stability to the ship as a whole. I had had little trouble with the ship south to Narau from Capiné, for instance, though admittedly, the weather had been clear and unsullied by even the hint of a storm. The barges used for most of the trade up and down the length of the Seticau River are rarely larger than twenty feet in any direction, and there are no walls.

The river itself is wide enough for most of its length that one has to strain to see the opposite shore, but despite this it is not very deep, and in many places shallows become rapids, and the bargemen will lash everything down, people included, as they force their way through.

We reached Gorsau with the sun at our backs, the morning muggy and hot despite the quickening season. The docks of Gorsau were disappointingly small until Tap explained that these were only one of fifteen docking areas; when I considered how much river traffic there would need to be to justify that kind of capacity, I realized just how big a city Gorsau really was.

From the docks it was not possible to see the rest of the city. Set upon a series of low cliffs, where the sheer faces had given way in the past the people of Gorsau had build steep stairwells down to the river, and docks at their feet. When the city had first been founded, there had been only a single narrow path down to the river; now there were eighteen, though most of these were narrow and dangerous, enough so that only a fool or a very desperate man would brave them.

The cliffs themselves were said to be hollow, and I was told that off and on for nearly four thousand years the caves riddling the cliffs had been used as an enormous catacombs for the dead of the city. They were apparently still being used as such, despite the currently more popular practice of taking the dead to Searle above the Moare ith Ghelde to the south. This last, for a city as far away as Gorsau, was only an option for the rich, but there was no shortage of them in Gorsau, as with most of the cities of the Southern Protectorates.

Tap stood awkwardly beside me as we waited for the rest of the men and equipment to be unloaded from the barge we had come on. The horses were causing the bargemen no small trouble, and I was very glad I had not been required to assist. I did not think badly of Tap for the nervousness he showed plainly enough on his face. He knew a little of what was coming, if not as much as I, and it was to his credit or his cowardice that he feared it more than anticipated it—most of the conscripts from Narau, especially the younger ones, carried about with them a look of excitement, and I suspected the conscription had not been entirely unwilling for many of them.

Tap indicated with a thrust of his chin a trio of men making their way through the crowd towards us. "Looks like the welcome mat is being thrown to the dogs," Tap said sourly.

"What do you mean?"

"The old man there is Gotib Sos, one of the better Warlords to ever pass the examinations. He's worked for the current Protector a few times, and he's very, very good."

"Why does that worry you? I would think that would be a good thing. It cannot help to have an experienced hand handling Gorsau's defense, when it comes."

"No, it doesn't worry me, though there are rumors that he's taken a bribe once or twice. Not for anything important, or the Protector wouldn't be using him, but it's something to consider. What worries me is the other two. The one in the white is Shevin Gal—a journeyman Seer. I've seen him a few times. He is more powerful than many full members of the Conclave, and he's been known to do their dirty work. I don't trust him," Tap finished bluntly. "The third one's name I don't know, but I don't need to."

Tap nodded to indicate the third. "See the imprint of a hand on his face? He's one of the Protector's Hands. I can see being met by Gotib Sos, but the other two? I can't help but wonder if we're to be thrown to the dogs just as soon as they finish with the welcome mat."

Tap fell silent as by this time they had come close enough to hear anything he said. The old man, the Warlord, led the way, the other two following behind him. The Warlord stopped in front of us, bowing slightly to Tap, who nodded in return, eyes darting about uncomfortably. The Seer was staring intently at me, all but ignoring Tap.

"Good day, my lord," Gotib Sos said to Tap. He turned to me and gave me a slight nod. "And to you, messir. I hope there have been no delays, gentlemen?"

Tap shook his head quickly. "Not at all, Warlord. The last of the conscripts from my city should be arriving by late afternoon, or so I've been told."

Gotib Sos grimaced. "Conscripts. I warned the Protector it would do more harm than good."

The Seer took his eyes from me. His voice was low, stern. "They will serve as good fodder for the front lines, to keep down the casualties of the more valuable troops," he said.

Tap looked at him angrily. "Narau's citizens are not fodder for the front lines!" he said hotly. I put a hand on his arm, and he fell silent, flushing.

Gotib Sos noticed the exchange, moving his eyes to me. "I understand you will be responsible for certain allies. I would like to speak with you later to work out the details."

I inclined my head. "As you wish."

The Seer was looking at me again. "From the description I was given, you can only be Aspin. I am Shevin Gal, of the Conclave. I understand you seem to think yourself some kind of a Seer."

His attitude annoyed me. I smiled. "No. Better."

"You sound very confident."

"I am."

"Knowledge of a word of two does not make one a Seer," the Seer Shevin Gal said sternly. "It takes years of practice and considerable discipline. Not all make it. Most do not."

"I only know one of the Words of Power."

Shevin Gal's eyes searched me. "One?"

"It has been sufficient to my humble needs," I replied,

no humbleness at all in my tone.

Shevin Gal was silent for a time. "You realize it may take you years as an apprentice before the Conclave permits you to leave Heveith Talige."

I stiffened despite myself. "I am not a Seer, nor have I any intention of becoming one."

"Nevertheless, if you wish to use the Words of Power responsibly, even just the one you know, you will need guidance and discipline."

"You are mistaken, I regret to say," I said, unable to keep a slight chill from my words. "When I am done assisting in the defense of Gorsau, I intend to return to Moage ith Gheldrinennen. The City of the Necromancers."

"Moage ith Gheldrinennen is nothing but ruins," Shevin Gal said, eyes suddenly hard. "And the Conclave intends that it remain so."

"We will see."

Gotib Sos cleared his throat. "If the messirs are done posturing like cocks in a ring?" the Warlord said. "We have much to do, and I would appreciate it if the Conclave would refrain from what it feels its duties are until the current situation is satisfactorily resolved."

Shevin Gal bowed. "Of course. You have my word."

"Good." Gotib Sos glanced back at Tap. "My lord, one of my officers will be along shortly to take over the management of your troops. Please ensure that there will be no problems." Tap inclined his head, and Gotib Sos continued. "I, for one, have work to do, if we are to get this army moved in time to do any good."

Shevin Gal spoke up. "Perhaps Messir Aspin would care to join me at a tavern I know of. I would be interested in getting to know him better."

I forced my lips into a thin smile. "I would be delighted," I replied.

Shevin Gal pretended not to notice, nodding his head to indicate that I should accompany him. I followed Shevin Gal from the docks up a set of steep stairs ascending the cliff. It was not an easy climb, and I did not envy the dock workers of Gorsau for having to haul supplies up the steps. As I found out later, they generally did not have to, as they had long since come up with a system of winches to bring bulk supplies up and down the cliff face. Shevin Gal led me through a maze of buildings at the crest of the cliffs, at last pausing before a low row of buildings set a ways back from the edge of the cliff and behind several other rows of construction.

"Not exactly high class," I commented.

Shevin Gal did not seem to take offense. "There are other taverns, but this one is closer."

"Closer to what?" I said, narrowing my eyes. "The docks?"

"Patience. All will be explained," he replied cryptically. Shevin Gal led me into one of the buildings, a rundown tavern or winehouse with a urinating stallion on the sign outside the door.

I eyed the sign. "Charming," I said dryly. "Do you take your friends here as well?"

The Seer ducked into the tavern, turning to me as I followed him inside. "I have no friends." His eyes quickly roved the smoky interior, at last settling on a middle-aged man with a scraggly beard and the beginnings of what was becoming of most formidable paunch. "Messir, I would like to take advantage of your back room," he said, smoothly depositing a few coins into the tavernkeeper's hand. Business concluded, Shevin Gal bowed his head slightly, indicating for me to precede him into the room.

The room beyond was not large, barely more than ten feet across, and the table in its center was exceeded in its distinct lack of quality only by the chairs surrounding it. Signs of repair were evident, and there were what looked like bloodstains on one of the walls, but the smoke was only a faint remnant here rather than the all pervading cloak that it was outside in the common room. Shevin Gal took one of the chairs for himself, the one farthest from the door, and I took the one opposite him, not really wanting to be any closer to him than was absolutely necessary.

Shevin Gal folded his hands carefully in front of him on the table, looking across the table at me with fathomless eyes. "There will be drinks brought in momentarily," he said, as if anticipating my question. "I may be only a journeyman, but be assured that I speak and act in the interests of the Conclave. They know what I am doing, and approve of it. The Words of Power are our most sacred responsibility, and when we heard of one who was raising the dead in the east, it was first thought that perhaps you were merely a renegade Seer. Such do surface from time to time, but they are never permitted to do much harm. Our reputation and purpose are threatened by such random exercises of power."

The tavernkeeper entered, placing two large mugs of some substance that might kindly be called liquor in front of us. Shevin Gal turned to the tavernkeeper before the man could leave. "There will be a couple of others joining us later. Please be so good as to let them in." The tavernkeeper grunted and left.

I watched Shevin Gal with quizzical eyes. "Others?" I questioned.

Shevin Gal held up a hand. "Patience. All will become known soon enough." The Seer lifted the mug in front of him to his lips, apparently choosing to ignore that I had not touched the mug in front of me. I did not fully trust this man, but I was curious as to his purpose.

"And so, Messir Aspin, we then determined that in fact you were not a Seer, renegade or otherwise. This presented the Conclave with something of a dilemma. You were clearly not a Thaumaturge—they are little more than foolish old men in any event—and it was certain that you were no Seer, either. Some suggested that perhaps you were the apprentice of one of our dark brethren, but most thought this unlikely. The center of the Dark Seers' power is at Toadebregane Hoge, and that is far from the reports of your actions. Besides, they seem more concerned with hiding who and what they are than in doing anything meaningful; they have long since abandoned the true search for knowledge that was their birthright."

Shevin Gal pushed the mug away from him, pressing his hands down on the table as he leaned over it to me. "Who taught you?" he asked intently. "The Necromancers are gone. We are sure of that. Six hundred years ago,

Moage ith Gheldrinennen was burned to the ground, the earth salted where it had stood. None survived. For a hundred years we scoured the land to ensure that none of that ilk had survived to spread their evil again."

"You are quick to call my necromancy evil, for one whom even the nobles distrust and hold at arm's length."

A brief flash of something that might have been anger flashed in Shevin Gal's eyes. "Ignorant peasants," he stated. "Fools. We do what is necessary. If they cannot understand the value in what we do, they stay out of our way or pay the consequences."

"And the Protector? Will he, too, pay the consequences?" I asked, eyes meeting his unblinkingly.

Shevin Gal relaxed, leaning back, his eyes still locked with mine. "The Protector is the master of the Protectorates," he replied, as if that concluded the issue. "But that does not address my question, which you have not as yet answered. Who taught you?"

I snorted. "And I should tell you so you can find him and stamp him out? I don't think so."

Shevin Gal narrowed his eyes. "You will not tell me who he is, then?" The air in the room had suddenly become still.

I laughed. "No. I'll tell you. But it won't do you any good. It was a god."

Shevin Gal did not register his reaction on his face, but I could almost see his mind working as he sat there. At last he nodded. "Yes, that makes sense. It is easier to believe than that the tradition survived for six hundred years under our noses." He grimaced. At that moment he looked behind me. "So good of you to join me, messirs." His lips moved then, but I could hear nothing of what word he murmured under his breath.

I tried to turn, only then hearing the rough laughter and sounds of two men behind me, but my muscles were locked in place and I was unable to move. My eyes widened as I stared at Shevin Gal who was shaking his head.

"Foolish boy," he said. "You believe in your own power and yet do not believe in mine. There are other Words of Power than the Seven, and you should listen

169

more carefully when a Seer invites you to a room where none others can listen. It is a pity, but we cannot take the chance that you might rebuild the Moare ith Ghelde. Since you are the only one who needs to be disposed of, this will make matters relatively simple."

One of the men behind me suddenly reached forward around my head, calloused hands tying a gag around my mouth. Shevin Gal's eyes turned hard as he looked at the men behind me. "The immobility will wear off in a few hours, but that should be more than enough time to do what needs to be done. Carry him to the caves and slit his throat there. No one will find him there until it is far too late, and I do not want this place connected to his death in case anyone saw us enter together." Shevin Gal took one last look at me. "And you will not be able to usurp the Seers' rightful position by playing at games best left to those of greater discipline than you."

One of the thugs forced a hood over my head, and together they lifted me out of the chair, stringing me between them as if I had passed out from too much drink. Shevin Gal opened the door and waited until they had dragged me out before exiting himself, apologizing wryly to the crowd and making a joke about his "brother's" lack of ability to hold his drink.

The crowd laughed appreciatively, and then a blast of cool air hit me as I was unceremoniously hauled outside. It was probably close to half an hour later when the sounds of the city faded to silence, the strenuous grunts of my companions as they manhandled me around.

"Here. This is good enough," one of them said.

"No. A little further. He might scream."

"That's what the gag's for, idiot." They dropped me on the ground, my muscles aching in pain. One of them ripped the hood off of me.

"I'm not going to waste a perfectly good hood," the second man explained defensively.

"I didn't say a thing." The first man peered down at me, his features all but invisible in the darkness. "So, you're a Necromancer, eh? You don't look like much to me." He gave me a sharp kick in the ribs. "Didn't like that? Here, try

170

this." He kicked me again, this time in the groin. Tears came to my eyes at the pain, but I could not move a muscle with the Seer's work still on me and the gag still stuffed down my throat. My strangled choking seemed to amuse the first man immensely; the other just looked nervous.

"Let's get this over with," he insisted. "I don't like it down here."

The first man shot a disgusted look at his companion. "Weakling. The dead are dead."

"They may not stay that way for *him*."

"He's not going to be doing anything gagged and with his throat cut, fool."

"Then do it, and get it over with." He shivered. "I want to get out of here."

The first man drew a knife from his belt. "This will hurt a bit, I imagine," he said to me. He lowered the knife to my throat.

23

We say we value trust, but I think it is rare that we truly know what we mean when we say that we do. I trust my brother, says one man, and at the word of the other, the one walks into what he believes is certain death. I trust this man, says another, and he believes this man, though his friends say he is a fool.

Trust is valued because it is rare. If it were not for the pain of all the betrayals of the world, there could be no pride in the trust given by one to another. When I lay helpless in the caves of Gorsau, I was closer to the second man than the first, and in that moment I knew myself for a fool. I waited for the knife to cut my throat, and knew there could be no redemption.

But if life can be a strange thing, death may be stranger still.

The second man gave a strangled cry, and the first man paused, his knife beading a thin line of red across my throat.

The first looked up, impatient, then his eyes widened as well. My face was facing the other direction, away from whatever it was that they saw, but the look of sudden fear on the first man's face told me what I needed to know, though not how.

"Go!" the voice breathed. "Go, now. He is mine, mine. Flee, and I will let you leave, else I will bring you to join with me in the place where I reside."

"Who are you?" the second man gasped, stumbling backwards, tripping over my Seer-bound body.

"Call me the black-eyed snake who bites your heel, call me the plague that fells the guilty while leaving the innocent unharmed. Call me all of these, and call me vengeance. Call me vengeance upon the justice of the land!"

My captors fled, and I waited.

"Aspin, why have you let them do this to you?" she whispered.

I wanted to answer, but could not, for the gag still held my lips firm, and the Seer's magic bound my limbs faster than any twine or metal circlets. I watched her, faint in the dying light of the cave, took what was her into my eyes so that I would never forget.

I was silent for hours more, in the darkness, waiting there with only the drip, drip of some forlorn trickle of water flowing through the caves to keep me company. Soraliangila had left, gone to wherever it was that she waited that was neither the Second World nor the Third, leaving me alone with the power of the Seer's charm tingling in my limbs.

I wondered if the men would come back, if they would tell the Seer what had happened; I wondered if he would believe it if they told him. In their place I knew that I would not have told Shevin Gal, for as far as they knew I was dead, eaten or driven mad by some ghost or revenant dwelling beneath Gorsau in caves measureless to man.

The feeling returned to my fingers and legs only slowly, a bit at a time. I lay on my side, tortured muscles straining to lift themselves up. The faint light that had seeped in from some high gallery had vanished but for a feeble glow, and I thought it might be night. At last I was able to pull away the gag, and I stayed there upon the hard rock for a long time, dragging the humid air into lungs starved for sustenance. I pushed myself to my knees, feeling along the floor until I found a wall, and leaning against it I dragged myself to my feet.

Shevin Gal had said the Word would wear off in a few hours, but it seemed to have been much longer. My throat was dry and my stomach aching, and above, I knew Baron Sevon's army must be at Gorsau's gates. Tap Seridius would be with his men, fighting horrors that knew no mercy and would never give any quarter. I felt long dormant lines within me writhe, and knew the Sergeant and the others were close, very close, but there would be almost ten thousand in Baron Sevon's host, and maybe more.

Ten thousand against Gotib Sos' sixty, but for all that, Gorsau was doomed, even if it was I alone who knew it. Five hundred demons had broken my fifteen hundred once already, and I had no illusions that they could do the same again. Fifteen hundred of the dead would stem the tide, but even they could not break it, not without a hundred times that.

I stopped, and there in the darkness, listened to the beat of my heart as it stirred in my chest.

A hundred times that. How long had the people of Gorsau been putting their dead in these caves? I tried to laugh, but the sound came out a harsh mockery of my voice, but even so, it was beautiful. Ironic, I thought, that Shevin Gal should hand to me on a platter the solution I needed. I pushed myself off the wall, concentrating on keeping ill-used legs steady and standing.

How long? I started moving, walking slowly, deeper into the caves. When I judged I had gone far enough, with my throat raw and broken I called out a Word, and I waited.

They came, in their hundreds and thousands, crowding the corridor. I felt a faint glimmer of fear rise in my breast, quickly banished as the lines of power rose and swelled within me like a flood. *This* was power, power to do with what I willed. But even as the thought came it ebbed as I brutally forced it down. I had been seduced once, but I knew it now for what it was, and would not make the same error twice.

As the dead came to me, I waited until they had come as close as they could. At their head came a tall wraith, crowned in the glory of a king. His beard was fierce white, and upon his back he bore a great sword the likes of which I had never seen. Cold eyes worn down by ageless eons regarded me.

"Who calls us from our resting place? *Who calls us?*"

"I come to you in the steps of Arnomoare Nimasgheld, and I would ask of you and yours only that which is yours to give, should you choose to bestow it upon your children."

The old king frowned. "I do not know that name."

I felt a faint chill sweep through me. "When did you last walk upon the earth?" I whispered.

"It has been a long time, a very long time," he said "What year is it, boy?" I answered him, and the old king was still for a moment. "Then it has been almost four

174

thousand years since I last stood beneath the sun in this city that was mine, and my father's before me, since my sire came out from the south to conquer those who dwelt here before, and make this place his own." He paused again. "I had not thought it would be so long."

I swallowed my nervousness and bowed. "My lord, there are others who have come to this place, to plunder this city. They are not human, but spirits ripped from the world that comes before this one. They have swallowed the north already, and now wish to swallow the south. They come in their thousands, and each will strike down ten or twenty men before it falls, and there are not now those twenty or even ten men to face them. This city will fall, and all before it. I would ask your help, in the name of your children, who do not know how. I have no right to demand this of you, and so I ask it of you."

The old king regarded me with cold fire in his eyes, and when he spoke, his words echoed in my skull. "No right?" he demanded. "No right? You came when no other would, dared what no other could, and you tell me you have no right? Had I known it had been so long, I would have come even had you not spoken the Word." The old king looked contemptuously at those around him. "Perhaps these others needed the Word, but not I. Come, boy, or I should say man, and let us aid these, my children's children!"

The umbra drew the phantom blade, and as one we marched from the caves.

175

24

When is the past gone, and the forgotten forgotten? When does a lost thing become lost, and a found thing found?

It is not always enough that I say the Word. There must be *need,* or else the other may be as nothing. Ten years dead, or twenty, or even a hundred, they will all come at my call whether they will or not, but a thousand? *Four* thousand? There is barely dust when those there have lain in the ground that long, yet still they came.

A wraith is not a corpse, and it cannot stay longer than it wills. A single night, perhaps, or a dozen, flickering in and out for a moment here or there until at last its time is spent, its will dried up and gone.

It was not my need that had called them, the dead under Gorsau, but it was my voice that showed the way.

We emerged on one of the fifteen little alcoves of shambled rock that the people of Gorsau used as docks. The sun above was bright, but the sky was smudged with smoke. A line of warehouses and whorehouses ran parallel to the docks, but the docks themselves were empty of ships, and both warehouses and whorehouses as empty of their usual clientele. The old king turned to me as we entered into the places of the living.

"I do not know this place."

"It has been four thousand years. There are docks all along the river now. Those steps lead up to the city itself," I replied, pointing the way.

"Ah. In my time, there was but one dock. Lead on, boy."

I nodded soberly, glancing once at the gathering host behind us, and started up the stairs. The old king rose faster than I, the ghosts and shades of his blood-kin swirling after him, around me and about me until I was choking in the grave scent of dead come again mixed with the sickly sweet smoke of a city afire. The city convulsed in the grip of chaos as we reached the heights.

Men and women with children rushed through the streets, all but the oldest men and the women bearing whatever makeshift arms they could find. The wide boulevard was crowded with the litter of looted homes, the spent seed of animals who hide in the skins of men.

But the city held despite the ragged fires set by opportunists thinking to benefit from the tumult, and as my host marched through Gorsau towards the landward gate the people fled in terror, mothers clutching babes to their arms as the dead rose, and walked. A hundred passed up the stairs, and then two hundred, and three and four. A thousand passed, and still more came.

The streets were clogged with the dead of four thousand years, ghost and shade and shadow and walking corpse, all of that which had ever been Gorsau.

We reached the landward gate, the walls above crowded with the Protectorate soldiers and conscripts bearing short bows and pikes. The gate shuddered and groaned as a ram hit it, and the smell of burning pitch choked the air as fire lit up the sky outside the walls.

I stood before the gate, the Protectorate soldiers looking down upon me in fear. The old king by my side waited. My eyes ran across the parapets until I picked out a familiar figure. "Warlord!" I shouted.

Gotib Sos's crisp manner appeared unchanged, but something lurked deep in his eyes that even I could see, a hollowed bleakness now that he could see the nature of the force arrayed before him. He saw me, gaze fixing on me where I stood.

"Open the gates," I called up to him. "I have an old score to settle with the Baron." Gotib Sos hesitated only a moment longer, his eyes taking in the vast host arrayed behind me before ordering two soldiers to open the gate. The landward gate's catches were released, and the heavy doors crashed inward, the wood splintering along one side.

And there, above the scent of smoke and the charnel of the wasting yard, I smelled rotting flowers.

Demon hound and demons in human form did not even register surprise at the sudden collapse of the doors. Launching forward, they howled with the hunger of those who do not fear the loss of simple flesh and bone, and I

177

fought nerves scraped raw with thirst and fatigue not to flee. The old king snarled beside me. "This is *my* city." And the dead swept forward.

What is the sound of revenant's blade upon flesh and bone, whatever the nature of the soul that lurks within it? The demons twisted and writhed as they snapped and tore at the phantom figures dancing around them, the ethereal chill slowing their rabid frenzy and sapping the strength from them. The spites and shades so occupied, the lumbering mass of corporeal dead arrived, and if they were only a fraction of the total number of the old king's host, still they outnumbered those they faced.

There is nothing glorious about war. There is blood and bone, and the only salve I could lend to my sickened senses were that this time, at least, the only ones who would die were those who had died already, in mind if not in body as well. As the old king's host overwhelmed the Baron's army, the dead crumpled with the splinter of bone and pulsified flesh. The fall of every dead sent a shot of nausea through me. Ruthlessly I cut off each, cauterizing it within me as soon as it snapped; there could be no time for grief or remorse, and I could not afford the pain trying to maintain their hold on this world would take. There would be no point, as even at my strongest I could not hold them all to this place.

Still the dead poured through the gates, their bodies burying Baron Sevon's demonic host, but there were so many more of them than the Baron's that it did not seem to matter. From far above on the walls, someone was sounding a horn, and in the distance I thought I could hear another answer.

The demonic host clawed and hungered like a mad beast knowing no terror, no fear, no thought of retreat, and there in the center of the maelstrom I suddenly saw a platform borne on the shoulders of four ghoulish men, and upon the platform stood the armored form of Baron Sevon. A sword of black iron was in one hand, and shield strapped to the other and a helm on his brow. Snarling, he lashed out from his makeshift dais, flecks of saliva running down his chin. As I watched his eyes locked on me, and for a brief moment he paused, and then he launched into motion, almost beheading one of his bearers in his haste to reach me.

The tide of dead seemed endless, and still it came. It pushed out through the gates and into the Baron's host, and through sheer weight of numbers it made any forward advance by the Baron all but impossible. I saw his sword lash out, and this time it did take the head of one of his bearers. The bearer stumbled, the other three fighting to keep the platform aloft, but the Baron fell into the storm of metal and bone, and was seen no more.

The earth beyond the landward gate of Gorsau was a square mile of charnel yard. Ravens and crows circled above, waiting for the last of the battle to cease so that they could begin their grim feast. A single long column of soldiers wound their way about the pockets of fighting still going on, their banners sputtering in the wind of their passage. At their head rode a body of cavalry, light lances held aloft, swords still sheathed.

When they reached me the line ground to a halt, and one of the riders dismounted slowly and walked towards me. "Aspin."

"Sergeant. It's good to see you."

The Sergeant chuckled, and, for once, it felt right to hear a dead man laugh. "Yes."

Two figures moved towards me, one lanky, thin hair slick with blood and sweat upon his forehead, the other short, broad shoulders and stolid expression somehow fitting on a man with the red imprint of a hand on the left side of his face. The Sergeant waited on the knoll with me, twenty of my bodyguard ranging around the base of the swelling in the earth, a mark to the fact that the Baron's body had not been found, and if he still lived, he would hunger for me.

Tap Seridius seemed nervous, but the sword he wore at his side had the look of one recently used despite the gilt and inlay upon the scabbard. The other man might as well have been rock for all the emotion he showed facing the wights at the base of the hill.

After a moment two of the twenty preceded them up,

another two falling behind. When they reached the top of the knoll, Tap licked his lips. "Aspin?"

"Hello, Tap," I said.

Tap's eyes flickered over to his companion. "Aspin, the Protector's Hand wanted to speak with you. I told him I thought you would see me, but I wasn't sure if you would see him. I hope that was all right."

"It's all right. Don't worry, Tap." I took in the way he stood, the fatigue in the way he stood, face drained of strength. "How many?"

Tap shrugged, but the casual gesture did nothing to hide the pain in his eyes. "Twelve. We were lucky. Narau's were not among Gotib Sos' expeditionary force. The others were not so lucky."

I glanced at his weapon. "I thought you were on the walls." "I was, but somehow demons got into the city." Tap paused. "One of them tried to take my head with him as a trophy. I decided I had better places to see than the type of place he was likely to want to visit."

"Your weapons master would be impressed. I am."

Tap forced a small grin to his lips. "I may be little more than a body attached to the lips assigned by the guildhalls to kiss the Protector's ass, but my uncle had money enough to afford a halfway decent master to teach me what I could learn."

The stocky man shook his head. "The Protector will hear of what you have done, and I do not mean the slaying of that thing. I do not think you will remain a tool of the merchants' associations forever." He turned to me. "Messir Aspin. It is perhaps necessary that we speak now."

The Sergeant watched the stocky man, but if he was aware of that one's gaze he gave no sign.

"Do you have a name?" I asked.

"Call me Tolbe," he replied, and I thought I detected the faintest hint of a smile.

I smiled in recognition of the joke. "The Hand. Appropriate, and certainly descriptive."

"It serves the purpose when one must be had. Messir Aspin, it was thought that something like this might happen. It was not, however, expected that it would

180

happen before you had a chance to speak with the Protector himself."

"Shevin Gal."

"Yes. The Seer is well known to the Protector's Eyes as the lackey of the Conclave, and their 'assignment' of him to this venture we took merely as an information gathering expedition. It was not anticipated that he would move immediately upon you."

My eyes found Tolbe's, and his held mine steadily, unwavering. "Then you knew."

"Yes. We knew. And did nothing."

I felt emotions warring within me. "Some might be offended," I said at last.

"Some might," Tolbe acknowledged. "But my duty, my *responsibility,* is to the Protector." He paused. "Not to you. I do not mean offense by this, only to clarify to you that there was nothing personal in my actions, or lack thereof."

"I know about duties. I do not hold yours against you. However, know that Shevin Gal has started something that may fall to me to finish."

Tolbe bowed slightly. "I respect what you have done for the Southern Protectorates and Gorsau today, and so I will apply candor rather than cruder means in what I require. The Protector would speak with you, regarding your intentions. It is in his interest to know the powers that are. The Thaumaturges care for nothing but their own pursuits, the Dark Seers hunt upon forgotten paths seeking a lost glory that never truly was, and the Seers plot and scheme in Heveith Talige. But you, he does not know about. What do the Necromancers want?"

"And if I decline your . . . invitation?"

"Then I will attempt other means. It is nothing personal," Tolbe answered, unperturbed by my apparent refusal.

I nodded. "I understand."

"Will you then come?"

"I will think about it."

Tolbe bowed again, and turned, making his way back down the knoll.

Tap glanced at the Sergeant hesitantly. "Do they know

what we are saying?" he asked me in hushed tones.

I glanced at the Sergeant.

The Sergeant replied, "I hear you, lord."

Tap turned to look at the wight. "What is it like there, beyond the veil?" he asked. "Is there much pain?"

"The ocean, and the sky. And everything in between. Go now, lord. Your people will have need of you."

Tap nodded, and went the way of the Protector's Hand.

"What did you mean by that, Sergeant?" I asked.

"There is something inside of you that there was not when we last parted," the Sergeant said.

I looked away, not wanting to meet his gaze. "Yes. More than you can know."

"Will you go to this Protector?"

I was silent for a long time, not knowing how to answer. "Yes. But there is something I must do first."
The Sergeant waited. I steeled myself, looking after the departing figures of Tolbe and Tap Seridius. "I must lay some ghosts to rest that should never have been risen."

"The gray king's host has returned to their biers."

"I know. They are not whom I mean."

The Sergeant said nothing.

Interlude

To His Excellency, Messir Tolbe of Shaur:

Greetings. I regret that I am unable to deliver this message to you personally, but there are matters beyond my immediate control that must take precedence. I wish to assure you and the Protector that I would be honored to visit him in Shaur and will do so as soon as I complete certain other business that requires my attention. I expect to be able to join you in Shaur before another fortnight is spent, and will await your pleasure and that of your master at that time.

Respectfully,
Aspin of Asperine

25

They waited for me in a forested vale on the southern shore of the Seticau River some twelve miles upstream of Gorsau. Gotib Sos had loaned me the use of ferries to move my men across the river, and in the early morning after the Battle of Gorsau I said my good-byes to Tap Seridius.

"Where will you go now?" Tap had asked.

"To run an errand, first, and to Shaur, to keep an appointment there. And then, to Searle."

"You mean the Moare ith Ghelde, don't you."

"Yes. I have put it off for too long."

"Only the dead go there."

"I suppose I shall be in good company, then."

Tap grasped my arm, eyes catching mine. "Farewell. I will miss you."

"You have your own people to take care of," I replied gently. "They will need you."

"Will they come again, Aspin?"

"Someday. Unless they are stopped."

Tap looked down, not meeting my eyes. "The Protector will never send an army north."

"I know."

"They will not make the same mistake twice. Next time, they will come with spies and saboteurs, and turn us against each other," Tap said with sudden emotion. "The others are fools, and they will listen to their blandishments, their lies and rotting promises."

"I know."

"Then we are doomed. The Seers will not help us."

"No. There is a way."

"What is it?"

"I cannot tell you. Not yet. You will have to trust me."

"I do, and I will."

"Good luck, Tap. And thank you."

From one of the horses lying dead on the battlefield I had liberated a proper mount. Tolbe watched me as I rode onto the ferry.

"I have not forgotten my promise," I told him.

184

Tolbe's eyes held mine. "Do not be too long. I will delay the Protector as long as I can, but he is not a man of infinite patience."

"I will do what I can."

Tolbe nodded, and turned and left.

They waited for me in a forested vale on the southern shore of the Seticau River some twelve miles upstream of Gorsau. The Sergeant followed me as I gathered rations from the stocks I had borrowed from Gorsau's stores.

"Where are you going?"

I looked up. "To be alone, Sergeant. For a little while. And then to do what I should have done before."

"I will go with you."

I shook my head. "That's all right. I will be better alone."

The Sergeant stepped in front of me, rotted, eyeless face a foot from my own. I stopped in astonishment. "I have abandoned you twice already. I will not abandon you a third time!" he said, slurring his words in his vehemence.

"I do not need your help!" I replied angrily, taking a step backwards. "Why do you care, anyways?"

The Sergeant stepped back, the sudden fury draining out of him. "Do not ask me that," he said with a curious lack of emotion I could not quite place. "There are some things that are better not known."

"I am not a child," I said from between clenched teeth. "And it is far too late for the succor of innocence." The Sergeant turned and walked away, and my own pique failed me as I stood there awkwardly, a loaf of drybread in my hand.

I rode into the high places above the vale, beyond where I could not see the company, though I could not erase from my mind the thin lines of vitality connecting us. I dismounted near a solitary oak on a peak, and walked the rest of the way to the top.

I looked over the dry grass of the hills, oaks spotting them in gullies lit by shallow, quick-moving streams. I came down the hill, leaving my mount behind, and walked until I was tired, and then I sat down. I turned my eyes upwards to the sky, but I could not make myself say the Word.

For seven days I waited, eating only a little, drinking just enough to keep me alive. It rained on the sixth day, and I sat in the warm rain, willing it to wash away my own human frailties.

On the dawn of the seventh day, I stood, and I whispered a name, and then a Word.

She came to me, flickering across the hillside until she was so close I could have touched her. I lifted a trembling hand, then let it fall. "It is done, Sora." She watched me, saying nothing, and I felt a wave of uncertainty. "It is not fair that you should haunt this world."

"I am no spite or shade summoned by you. You cannot send me away, Aspin."

"I know." I steeled my heart and said the words that needed to be said though they tore at me to utter them aloud. "You must go, and never return. I cannot go forward while I still look backwards."

"Do you love me?"

"I do."

"Then why do you ask me to go?" she said.

I clenched my fists uselessly at my side. "Because I cannot let you go until you are gone, and seeing you like this is tearing me apart. Can't you understand?" I cried, anguish in my voice. "I want so much to ask you to stay, to have you here by my side, but I know it can never truly be, and that sooner or later it will drive me mad. You showed me the way, and now I must take it, but I must walk it alone. In the places I must go, I cannot afford to look back, and that is all I can do when I know you are with me, even when I cannot see you."

Soraliangila flickered in the shadows cast by the newborn sun. She bowed her head, turning as she faded, her hand raised to her face. My heart clenched spasmodically, and I opened my mouth to call out to her, to take it back, but then she turned back, and her eyes met mine.

And then she was gone.

I raised a cairn upon the height of the knoll beneath an oak tree that looked to have stood there four hundred years. Someday, it would fall, but until then it would give a sheltering shade to a memory that I knew I would carry with me until I died, however I might try to leave it there behind me under the stones piled high.

We carry our mistakes with us no matter how we try to leave them behind. If they color our actions and our words and deeds then they are not forgotten, though we do not summon them into the witness of those societies in which we dwell. The days are brighter, and the nights darker, and we grow a little older each day.

We marched west and south, away from the river and into the dry hill country of the western Protectorates still east of Shaur.

Shaur lay on a half dozen muddy islands upon the flat waterplain that flowed as a tributary out of the main branch of the Seticau River. Trade ran up and down the river and west to the mines in the Red Hills and south to Searle, but the greatest part of the trade was not in goods but in the machinery of the Protectorate bureaucracy. The city itself was technically a sovereign state in its own right, apart from being the residence of the Protectorate, and in fact it did maintain its own set of offices and governors, but it was not accident that many of Shaur's civil officers also bore comparative Protectorate titles and duties, and it was rare that an officer would choose to flaunt his civic titles over his Protectorate titles.

In most places in the south I had been the Protector was a distant thing, a convenient political fiction that allowed for certain advantages in trade and common defense, but if you asked a man in, say, Medennen or Narau where he hailed from, he would not say the Southern Protectorates, but Medennen or Narau; civic loyalties ran much deeper than Protectorate loyalties.

In every place but Shaur. There, it was the Southern Protectorates that kindled fire in men and women's hearts, and I sensed there as I made my way through the crowds near the eastern gate a nascent excitement that I had not seen in the other cities. In Shaur, you would hear people say, even a beggar could live like a king if he used his wits and courted the favor of the Fifty True Gods and the Twenty Lords of Light.

187

Seers dressed in white moved through the crowds singly and in small groups, most often a master sitting in the Conclave followed after by two or three journeymen or apprentices. Glances followed them wherever they went, but none seemed to comment on their presence.

I had pulled back my own black cloak to reveal a deep green shirt Tap had given me, and for the most part the people ignored me. The dead I had left a mile outside of the city, but for the Sergeant and three others, and all of these I ordered bundle themselves in cloaks and cover their faces. I could do nothing for their smell, but as it turned out I doubt anybody would have noticed, for though Shaur had the underground sewers Narau had so pointedly lacked, the manure of sheep and horses graced the ground and mixed with the fragrant scents of the Butchers' Quarter and the numbing odor from the Dyers'.

I stopped to speak with a guard at one of the multitude of bridges linking the tiny islets making up the city by the simple expedient of planting myself in front of him and waiting until he had acknowledged my presence.

"I am looking for the residence of the Protector," I explained. "I have an appointment."

The guard looked me up and down, taking in the travel stains on my clothing and my guard, swathed as they were in heavy cloaks and hooded helms. "And my mother is the new lord of Medennen. Go away, *oatrin*."

"I am no tramp. Bring your captain to me, and let him decide."

"And why should I waste my time?"

"Because," I observed patiently, "if I am wrong, you will at best be made a fool of by your captain and lose your dignity. If I am right, you may well lose your head. It does not seem a bad bet to make to me."

The guard scowled and pointed to a broad circular building in the distance—the way I had just come, naturally. "It's that way. If they let you in, it is no doing of mine.".

I bowed. "Thank you." We made our way through the teeming crowds to the building. At the entrance we were stopped by a squad of guards led by an officer, his blue plumes rippling in the faint breeze whispering unheard

188

through the city under the sound of the tumult.

I introduced myself to him, and he sent a runner into the building. A few moments later, a beanpole of a bureaucrat came out, face creased in a frown as he looked down at me.

"You say you have an appointment, Messir Aspin?"

"More in the way of an invitation from one of the Protector's Hands in Gorsau. He called himself Tolbe."

The thin bureaucrat grunted. "Means nothing. Half of them use that name. What was it concerning?"

"An interview with the Protector."

The bureaucrat pursed his lips. "Indeed. Wait here." He turned and left.

One could almost see the wheels of the Protectorate bureaucracy working as first one petty official and then another passed me off to one another. Others came as we waited, some being turned away, but most entering with only a cursory glance at their papers. I have heard it said that if the Seven Domains was built on blood and bone, and Narau upon gold and jade, then Shaur was built with paper and ink, and this is not, I think, so very far from the truth.

At last a short man appeared at the gate with a red imprint upon the left side of his face, and for a moment I thought it was Tolbe. He looked me over for a moment, then nodded. "Come with me."

I followed him into a large hallway or corridor of sorts held up by spiraling pillars along its length and the history of the Southern Protectorates as told in dozens of small murals in alcoves framed by miniature pillars paced upon the wall. We walked in silence for some time until at last we came to a small room done completely in red. The Hand turned to me as we entered the room. "They will have to stay."

"The Protector?" I asked.

"It is required."

"I have no weapons."

"I know. I am not without eyes." The Hand did not smile, but I thought he might have just made a joke, feeble as it was. I chuckled in appreciation, but quietly in case I had mistaken his intent. He opened a door and held it for me.

The room beyond was in every way a complete contrast to the one I had left. Half covered with a roof and walls, half bare of both, we were, I thought, halfway or higher up the height of the Protector's residence. Where the room we had been in before had been lushly carpeted, this room was adorned in simple marble. The ceiling was tall enough for five men or more standing one atop the other, and it could have held three of the governor of Capiné's dancing hall had it wanted. As it was, it held a simple chair, three men and a woman.

At first I was not sure the woman was a woman, so similar to one of the men was she, but as I approached she and her immediate companion moved around the other two sinuously, smoothly like a knife cutting water. The man had no beard or moustache, and both wore a loose sort of pants and vest of red and yellow. The woman was pretty in a deadly sort of way, but not really attractive, for while I approve of a woman's bite, there was something not quite human about *this* woman.

Of the other two men, one was tall and dressed entirely in black leathers, a faded scar running across his neck, the other in a simple linen robe belted at the waist, what seemed to be a blindfold held across his eyes. The tall man eyed me like a hawk a chicken that has strayed out of the henyard, and of the strange man and woman, I received the distinct impression that both were wondering if I would be good to eat.

I bowed. "Protector. I understand you wished to speak with me."

"You will be Aspin, then." The blind man's voice was quiet and unhurried.

"I am."

"It has come to my attention that you are largely responsible for the fact that Gorsau still stands. For that I wished to thank you."

I bowed again, saying nothing. He could not see me, of course, but those damned hawks surrounding him could, and if my obeisance relaxed their nerves even a little bit I

190

would count my pride a fair sacrifice for my sanity. "It is nothing, Protector."

"Those who dwell in Heveith Talige were less than enthusiastic when word came of the victory at Gorsau. It is said that the cries of outrage could be heard echoing throughout the rest of the city." A brief smile touched the Protector's lips. "I, of course, did not hear them, but it is well known that I focus entirely too much on the affairs of the Protectorates."

I wondered how much he knew. I had assumed Tolbe to have sent word to him of what had happened, but suddenly I wondered. Were the Hands expected to function as Eyes as well? Logic would at first seem to indicate that such would make the most sense, but I thought then that there might be just as good reasons for keeping the two functions as separate as reasonably possible.

"It did come to my attention that some among the Conclave do not look forward to what I might do," I said carefully.

"And what might that be?" the Protector said, leaning forward slightly. The Dragons at his side—for that is what they were—tensed, and the tall man with eyes that would have fit better by far on a hawk than a man frowned deeply.

"I have no intention of inflicting harm of any sort upon the Southern Protectorates."

"Wisely said, but I wonder if you have said what I believe you to have said or what you have really said."

I shook my head. "Protector, I defended Gorsau. Is that not enough?" I asked.

The Protector sighed, turning away slightly. "In simpler times, yes, it would be. But we live in perilous times, and there are many who would dress themselves in sheep's clothing in order to get close enough to plunge a dagger into the heart of the Protectorates. It is not an honor to serve the Protectorates as I do, messir, but a burden, and any who would say otherwise are fools entertaining visions of childish grandeur rather than the sober judgements of rational men."

"If you believe that is so, then it seems there is little I can do to convince you otherwise." I shrugged.

"What will you do next?"

"What I must. I will go to Searle, if you will permit me, and from there, I will pass down the river with the dead."

"And then?"

"I have never been there myself, Protector," I replied. "I can hardly tell you how I will react to circumstances that are at best still unfamiliar to me."

The Protector smiled briefly again. "Elegantly said. But there are some things you can tell me, if you choose. Such as whether you intend to rebuild the Moage ith Gheldrinennen, the City of Necromancers."

"I don't know," I said truthfully. "It is something I have been thinking about for a long time now, but until I stand in that valley in the Red Hills, I do not think I will know. But I can tell you this: if I do choose to raise the Moage ith Gheldrinennen, it will not be tomorrow or the day after tomorrow. I think there are things I have yet to do. Maorg-mehl still waits in the North, and there is much I have done to make his path easier. Before I raise the Moage ith Gheldrinennen, if that is what I choose to do, I must face him and his with whatever I can bring to bear. I do not know if that provides you with the assurance you feel you need, but I am tired of dissembling and lying."

"It does not give me what I want," the Protector said. "But it gives me something I can live with. Your motives are your own, I think, and not those of the Protectorates. But I do not think you are an enemy, and it is possible we may serve similar purposes." He turned, the interview at a close, and the hawk-eyed man led me firmly out of the open hall.

We left the city that night after the gates had been closed. I spent the afternoon and the evening drinking in a tavern overlooking the river, though there were no windows on the inside and the common room was choked with smoke and the debris of human lives. It must have been a few hours after the sun had set when I felt strong hands lift me up from the puddle of bad liquor in which I lay. "What time is it?" I murmured.

"It is late, Aspin."

"You shouldn't be in here."

"They will not notice."

"I told you to stay with the others in the rooms," I muttered feebly, struggling to sit up straight.

The Sergeant was silent for a few moments. When he spoke, there was a strange note in his voice I had never heard before. "Come, Aspin. You have had enough. It is time."

I didn't resist when he hauled me to my feet. The tavernkeeper looked over, and the Sergeant said to me, "Give him your pouch. You do not need it."

A haze still muddled my head, but those words snapped me out of the worst of my stupor. "Yes. You're right." I pulled the pouch from my belt and dropped it on the table. "Keep it," I said shortly.

They did not want to let us out when we asked for them to open the gates, but now that the moment was upon me I did not want stay in the city any longer. I stepped forward to the sympathetic guard. "Do you know who I am?" I asked.

The guard looked at me, puzzled. "No."

The Sergeant and the others of my bodyguard moved forward behind me, their hoods falling from their faces. The guard paled and opened his mouth to call out.

"Open the gate."

The guard was a sensible fellow. He shouted to another of the guards to wake the lazy gateboys and if they didn't hurry, he'd scour the skin from their hides himself.

The road to Searle was pitted with deep grooves, some almost as high as my waist, mute evidence of the multitude of wagons had passed from here and other places to Searle, leaving behind their precious cargos, their sons and daughters, their fathers and mothers and grandfathers and grandmothers.

In the lands south of the Seticau River for five thousand years, long before the Southern Protectorates had existed in name or form, the dead had always been brought to Searle, high in its mountain
eyrie, to leave behind the refuse of a life.

The dead trailed behind me, fifteen hundred in arms, poorly cared for armor and weapons clinking in the mute scuffle of my silent troop. Beside me the Sergeant and my bodyguard rode, more often than not off the road itself when the going allowed for it, as it often did.

A crowd of crows and rooks circled above us, drawn by the scent of death, yet made uncertain by what they saw. They called to one another in shrill voices, occasionally one or two of the braver of their mob swooping down, only to scatter at the last minute when the target of their affections moved. They followed us for a day and a half, finally leaving when we moved out of their range.

The rumpled tenor of the land increased as we moved farther south into the tiny cousins of the Red Hills, and far ahead we could see the earth's own stone towers rising from the land like sentries in some ancient war, frozen for all time in stony carapaces.

I wondered what it might be like to wake those slumbering giants; I wondered if it were anything like when I had wakened those who followed in my footsteps. In other places I had heard tales of how at times the earth would tremble, and seeing the Red Hills for the first time in my life, I could well believe that such murmurings were but the stirrings of some silent army, held trapped beneath the hard ground, struggling through the mist of sleep to waken and take again to arms.

It took four days all spent and told for us to climb to the high valley of Searle, and in that entire time we passed or met no others. It might have been nothing more than that such saw us coming from afar and fled far enough from the road that we simply could not see them, but to me it seemed as if this were but an echo of the world to come, that here, on this path to the dead, all others but us had already come, and that the world of a hundred years from now would be a dead and empty thing, as bare and barren as the Third World itself.

We wound our way down into the valley, marking homesteads and scattered mills, each crouched like a hungry animal over one of the trickling streams that made their way down from the snow packed crests of the hills above. We passed a fieldhand working in a stand of trees gathering wood. He raised his hand to us as we approached, hailing us. I raised my own hand in tentative greeting, wondering if he had not seen the nature of those who followed me.

He climbed up to the road, pulling his gloves off as he came, tucking them beneath his belt. He looked down the line of dead behind me, but there was no fear on his face, no approbation. Instead of warming me, it made a chill run down my spine.

"It's been a long time since we've seen one of your kind here, lord," he said to me.

"You're not afraid?"

His face sobered. "This is Searle," he said simply. "Do y'think we haven't seen the dead before?" He glanced at the Sergeant, then back to me. "Though it's been a long time since we've seen much in the way of the walking sort. My grandfather said he saw a revenant once, of my grandmother, but I think he was probably lying, or else broken in the head. He was getting on his years, y'see. But y'never know."

"I . . . I wasn't planning on staying long," I said lamely, a bit unsettled.

He nodded. "I'm not surprised. The dead, they all go down the river eventually. The only difference between the living sort and the dead is that the living generally go feet first."

"Charming," I said dryly.

The fieldhand grinned. "No, don't y'go all batty on me. There's a path going down the whole way, though it's been a long, long time since anyone's been using it. The only reason it's still there at all is because he had it carved in stone, not trusting to a dirt path."

"He?"

"Arnomoare Nimasgheld, of course. Or so I've heard it said."

"Oh," I replied with all eloquence. "I see."

The fieldhand looked over his shoulder to the stand of trees he had been working in. "I need to be getting back to work, lord, but I wish you and yours well." He waved to me as he made his way back down the bank, and I felt strangely at peace.

"You do not fear what you see every day of your life," the Sergeant said beside me.

"No, you're wrong. You can." I straightened. "I have to go down there alone."

"I will not leave your side. There are those who could harm you there."

"The dead?" I shook my head. "It is the living I fear." I stopped. "Why do you care?" I asked. "You would not tell me before, but before I enter the lands of the dead, I want to know. Before I set my feet upon what could be the end of my time on this earth, I need to know. You, alone of all the others, have stood by me for something other than because you must. I am not blind; I can see it, but I do not understand it." I watched the wight intently. "Why?" I asked.

The wight I called the Sergeant looked away. "When I was younger, as young as you, I was a fool," he said in a dusky whisper. "I thought of nothing but the glory of battle, of the honor to be bought in blood. I joined a mercenary company in Mesepare, with the last of the coin I had managed to scrape together buying a merchant's second best sword. The captain of the company led us across the river, for there was strife in the Seven Domains, and where there is war and strife, there is always a need for men who will fight for coin. It was a war like any other, we thought. We were wrong.

"For two years I fought, never looking back, living a soldier's life. We diced and wenched in the towns we plundered, never wondering at the strangeness of the men we fought for. Only the captain seemed truly affected by it, and as the months wore on he grew paler, and a creeping sickness seemed to rot away at his insides until he was little more than the shell of a man. Every two months, a foul smelling man dressed in a filthy cloak would come to the captain and speak with him for a while before giving him a heavy pouch full of coin, and every time when he was gone, the captain would turn to drinking, and cuffing every man he could lay his hands on, and when the drink had gone its course, we would sometimes find him weeping over his cups when he thought no one to be looking.

"In a little town in Gourine Domain I met a merchant's daughter. We fell in love, and when the winter months came upon us next and the company was disbanded until spring, I married her and took her back with me to my homeland in Asperine. All through the winter I labored to build her a home, and when it was done, I left her, two months heavy with child.

"Through spring and summer and the fall of autumn we fought across half the domains of the old empire, my brothers and I, and when winter came again, I left eagerly, and when I left again in the spring, my merchant's daughter was again with child. For four years I lived this way, and yet each year, there was a greater pall flung over the company. The captain had withdrawn into the shattered husk of a man he had become, the lieutenant barely better. The coin was always on time, but the price it carried with it was known only much later. To a mercenary, the most important thing is the coin he is paid in. We were paid well, and considered ourselves luckier than the men we fought, who for the most part were not paid at all, being the conscripted levies of a dying empire. At Freecastle, we fought again, but at our sides fought things that seemed human but were not; we watched in terror as they tore at the dead in a frenzy of feeding, and wondered at the nature of the things we had allied ourselves with.

"At Freecastle, I found myself in battle with a man better than I. He was just a peasant, but there was a desperation in his eyes and those of his comrades that lent greater passion and fury than any we had ever been able to muster in our ranks. He wounded me twice, and the second time he struck me in the belly. I lasted until sunset, and the last thing I remember of then is crying out to my mother.

"I died upon that battlefield, and my last thoughts were of my family. Of my mother, my wife, and my children. And of them, a son named Aspin, who I had seen only twice, but loved as dearly as my wife."

197

The Sergeant lifted his empty sockets to me. We gazed at each other for a long time, and then I dismounted, careful not to touch him. My hands were trembling, and it was all I could do to keep the quaver from my voice. "Take care of them if I do not return," I said at last.

"You will, Aspin."

"Yes, I suppose I will. One way or another." I took a deep breath, and started down the end of the path I had been following since the day I saw the god in the wood, trying not to think of the father I was leaving behind.

26

Of the Southern Protectorates, Searle is the oldest. Searle does not have the high walls or towers vaulting into the sky of Shaur or Gorsau. It does not have the trade or great markets of Medennen and Lipannen and Botoco and Narau. It does not have the mines of Tarau, nor the vast fisheries of Larau in the Far Islands. It is tiny compared to all of these places, the largest of which numbers nearly a hundred thousand living creatures, even the smallest close to ten.

Searle has never, or so its elders have told me, numbered more than a eight hundred, and yet despite this, there are stone markings on the walls of the valley that record events known to have happened well over four thousand years ago. Five thousand years of continuous habitation, there in one of the numerous high valleys of the Red Hills that are the source of the Seticau River and hold within their deepest ravines the Moare ith Ghelde, the Land of Death.

The people of Searle are not merchants, but they do trade a little, mostly for things they cannot make from their own hands. The people of Searle are not farmers, though most have some small vegetable garden hidden away here or there. Neither are they herders, though many keep a few goats, and at least one family is uncommonly proud of their herd of almost a hundred sheep, though I never was able to figure out why this should impress anybody. What they have is the River, and to those who come to Searle from all over the lands south of the Sóage Waste, this is enough.

In the late winter and early spring in every city of the south but Gorsau (and for some, even there), the dead are held in low, half-submerged lodges or caverns if such are available, or simply wrapped in breechcloth and dropped in some snowbank somewhere, if the snow is deep and cold enough that year. When the rains stop and the roads attain some semblance of rigidity, barges heaped with the bodies of the dead from that year make their way upriver to Shaur (or down in the case of Tarau), and from Shaur, by wagon south to Searle, high up in the hills across the floodplain north and west of the Halanere, what the Nomads call the Ocean Grass. The dead are unloaded in Searle, and the bodies sent down the river from Searle's heights, south and down into the Moare ith Ghelde, where the City of Necromancers once stood, where the dead lie, and where some say, even now, Arnomoare Nimasgheld still walks.

In six hundred years, no living man or woman had entered the Moare ith Ghelde and returned sane. Few had dared, and of those, almost none returned, and those who returned lacked their wits, numbed by some terror they would not speak of. The ghosts of the Moare ith Ghelde, it seemed, were peculiarly persistent. Somehow, nobody seemed to spend much thought on the reason why.

And so I, a living man, entered the Land of the Dead.

The path the man on the outskirts of Searle had spoken of was crabbed and worn smooth with the tread of six hundred years of wind and rain. There were steps of a sort, though they did not seemed to be carved to any human dimensions, and a restless earth had shifted them, slanting them downwards and making the going slow since I had no desire to wind up with my body crushed from falling from the heights. Indeed, the stream that the bodies were traditionally sent down seemed more falls than stream, so steep was its descent. The path itself wound down beside the stream, at times veering away from it for a hundred or two hundred steps or so only to edge back towards it. I had begun my descent into the Moare ith Ghelde at dawn, but it soon became clear that I would not reach the bottom before sundown.

I made camp about two thirds of the way down from the heights on a step broader than most. I had a bedroll, and I laid it out, chewing slowly on the dried fruit and jerky the innkeeper and his wife (or perhaps daughter, I had not wanted to embarrass myself by asking which she was) had given me when he found out who I was and what I intended to do. Their reaction had been odd, at that. There was no attempt to warn me away from my descent, nor any fear when it became clear who—or what—I was. I

200

asked if there had been others like me, and they both shook their heads, but both had heard stories, and neither saw anything to fear in me. Somehow, it was exactly what I needed, for despite my expectations, I slept deeply the night I spent in Searle, and in the morning woke calm and ready to do what I had come to do.

Dawn came late to the valley, and the rounded hills climbing to the very sky blacked out the sun for the greater part of its ascent. The valley that Searle lay in was but a pinprick compared to the vast elongated cut that was the great valley within which the dead of a hundred cities and towns now called their home. Where Searle was perched high in the Red Hills, the Moage ith Ghelde was cut deep, so deep that I suspected that the lowest parts of it fell well below the surrounding terrain beyond the Red Hills on the plain the Nomads called the Ocean Grass.

The stream descending from Searle widened as it fell, and as the drop levelled off the stream became a small river cutting the long valley in two, and in the distance, I could make out a narrow lake beside rumpled fields tufted with gold and a sprinkling of green.

The descent ceased its vicious downward plunge at the end, gently merging into flatland at the floor of the vale, and by late morning the steps had vanished to be replaced with the remains of a much older road that was all but covered with dirt and dust.

Bodies swathed in cloth choked the stream, and bones littered banks and road alike. I had eaten about a quarter of the food I had brought the day before, and I had elected to go hungry rather than eat any more of it; I did not know what I had come here to find, but I suspected I would be gone a while, and I did not know if I would be able to find much I would be willing to eat in this place at the bottom of the world.

I walked for three days along the old road. What looked like crypts and monuments flanked it along either side at irregular intervals, and even when the road had turned away from the river or the river had turned away from the road I still found the remains of those who had come before, with little to tell me whether they had been living or dead when they had at last lain down to their final repose. The hills rose above me like giants, and from the base of the valley it was easy to see how this place had come to be associated with death; it seemed as if one had descended into hell, so far from the sky it was. I had heard there were other ways of entering the Moare ith Ghelde farther to the south, the Gates of the Dead, called the Bevagennen ith Gheldrinennen, and even farther south, the Tangle Wood.

The path joined another, much larger road at one point, one part of it continuing south along the same direction I had been following, the other east towards the eastern wall of the vale. I continued south. On the second day, I ate the last of the food I had brought with me. On the third, I came at last upon the scattered remains of the Moage ith Gheldrinennen.

The City of Necromancers.

I had known it had been razed, but the word had not prepared me to accept the sheer magnitude of the destruction that had been visited upon this enclave. The rotted husks of buildings lay broken, shattered beyond belief and scorched black in places as if burned from sheer spite, for surely no sane man would think there was value in torching unfeeling rock. The wind and rain in six centuries had piled caked dirt and gravel atop it, and in most places it was impossible to be certain that a city had ever been there. I walked among its broken halls, shaken more deeply than I wanted to admit.

Near the center of the desolation I stopped, and found my breath coming shallowly as I crouched, fingers running through the soft earth that had been deposited there over the lonely centuries since the city had fallen. *Wasted*, I thought. *All wasted. For nothing.* I stood, and knew I had come for nothing, for a shattered city, and a broken dream. My cheeks were wet, and I wanted to rage against the world for the cheap trick it had played on me.

There was no revelation waiting for me here, no Arnomoare Nimasgheld to teach me what I needed. There was only destruction here, and beside me, only the dead waited. Neither anger nor fury nor hopeless grief would give me what I wanted to know. I had come full circle; I had returned to the despair that had set my feet upon this, an empty path, a wasted life.

"I warned you, but you would not listen."

I turned. He stood half again the height of the tallest man I had known, and there was an odd knowing in his eyes that told me that it was no man I faced. "You."

"I," the god of the wood agreed. "Have you come to repent for the ill you have done? Is there, then, anything good that you have done since you took from me the Word in the wood?"

I straightened, stung. "I *took* nothing. You gave it to me, of your own free will. Or have you forgotten that already?" I retorted. "If there was ill done, I will not claim it to be your fault, but there can be little honor in standing there as you do, mocking a mortal. Or is that what gods do to entertain themselves?"

The god shook his head. "I did not come to taunt you."

"Why did you come, then?"

"To offer you to take back what was given." My hands were sweaty, and I could not will myself to meet the god's gaze. "I can take it all back, mortal. I cannot change what has been, it is true, but I can change what is, and what will be. I can do that, and I will, for you. But what was freely given must be freely returned, or not at all."

The god sighed. "You asked me if I told Arnomoare Nimasgheld what I told you, that no good would come of it, and I said you did not know what you asked. I see by your eyes that you know now. He chose not to give it up. Out of pride, or something else, I do not know, and that choice destroyed him. You will not find him here, for his bones lie unremarked among those of a thousand others on the forgotten battlefield in a forgotten city a hundred miles from here. No one will raise his shade; no one will bring him back. Some things even you cannot do. But this is still your choice. You can choose to give it up, to go back to being what you were. There is no dishonor, no shame in that," the god said.

The wind coaxed dust devils out of the refuse that

203

covered the city, and I looked out over its destruction, and sensed a faint *something* stir deep within me that I had not felt in a long time. I faced the god as a strange calm settled over me. Fear was gone, and pain, and only the memory of despair still lingered over me, and that was touched with the first glimmerings of something harder, something stronger that would never bend, but instead make itself stronger with each blow despair felled upon me.

"When I was a child," I said at last, "I lived in a child's world, full of a child's things. Now I am an adult, and I must live in an adult's world. Innocence cannot be regained, only the palest illusion of it. Should I let you take from me the memories and actions that are who I have become?"

I shook my head. "No, I will not surrender what was bought and paid for. I shed sweat and tears and blood to gain what I have gained, and I will not give that up, even if you could take back all of the death and misery and despair, all of the broken promises and shattered dreams. *They* have made me stronger. Wiser." I paused. "What you have given me you cannot truly take back. If I let you take the knowledge of the Word from my mind, you would take a part of me with you, and it would simply live on in another form, changed, but still alive. Alive, but bereft of the wisdom that might let it be used to some semblance of mercy."

The god met my gaze with his own eyes until at last he nodded.

"So be it." He turned as if to go, and then he paused. "There is something else you deserve to hear." I looked up. "Nimasgheld would have been proud."

"Thank you," I whispered.

And he was gone.

Epilogue

I don't know what I expected to find in the Moare ith Ghelde. Redemption, or justice, or perhaps revelation, or even Arnomoare Nimasgheld waiting there for me with open arms, or the Third World itself.

But what I found was something entirely different. I found purpose, and I found something else that I had not expected to find.

I found peace.

There is a superstition in the lands south of the Seticau River. They say that when the dead walk, the cocks will crow though it be night unending without hope of morning.

Eight days after the madman had gone over the falls into the Moare ith Ghelde, in Searle the cocks crowed, though the dawn was yet to come.

People threw open their shutters, eyes wide in the light of the newborn moon. From over the falls, there came a dull rumble that was nothing like the rushing of the stream. First one, then a thousand, a hundred thousand forms crested the heights, and at their head stood a man dressed in grey, his face set with the knowledge of one who has conquered the inner demons of his soul. For a moment he paused upon the crest, the dead flowing around him and for a moment, the moon flung down its light upon him, and the world was reflected in his eyes.